Mrs. (Eliza Elder) Brightwen

Inmates of My House and Garden

Mrs. (Eliza Elder) Brightwen

Inmates of My House and Garden

ISBN/EAN: 9783337069605

Printed in Europe, USA, Canada, Australia, Japan

Cover: Foto ©Andreas Hilbeck / pixelio.de

More available books at **www.hansebooks.com**

INMATES OF MY
HOUSE AND GARDEN

BY

MRS. BRIGHTWEN

Author of " Wild Nature Won by Kindness"

ILLUSTRATED BY THEO. CARRERAS

New York

MACMILLAN AND CO.

AND LONDON

1895

To

Miss ELEANOR ORMEROD

*Consulting Entomologist to the Royal Agricultural Society, and
Fellow of the Meteorological Society.*

DEAR MISS ORMEROD, —

For thirty years you have been a pioneer in the fields
of agricultural zoology and chemistry, and it may most truly be
said that no woman has ever done so much as you have to protect
agriculture against its natural enemies. In the special departments
to which you have devoted your life, it is universally admitted that
you are without a rival.

My little volumes do not compete with work so serious as yours,
yet you have gratified me with your commendation of their truthful-
ness, and you have permitted me the pleasure of dedicating to you
this one, in some chapters of which I deal with the classes which
are most familiar to yourself.

Believe me to be

Yours very sincerely,

ELIZA BRIGHTWEN.

THE GROVE, GREAT STANMORE.
June, 1895.

7

PREFACE.

NCOURAGED by the extremely kind reception which has been awarded to my previous books, and by the assurances, which have reached me from the most unexpected sources, that they have been found pleasant and profitable, I am venturing to offer to the same indulgent public a third collection of personal studies of natural history.

I recognise clearly that my little volumes have been received with so much favour, because, in spite of their simplicity and their lack of scientific importance, they are, so far as they go, original. That is to say, I have not much to give, but what I have is of my own gathering. I have not borrowed from other and cleverer writers, but have set down as plainly as I could what I have myself observed and experienced.

It is my privilege to be unusually well placed for the minute study of living creatures, and in that study I find a pleasure so intense that I long to attract others to the same well-spring of pleasure. Unpretending as are the chronicles of the inmates of my house and garden, they are scrupulously true, and every fact that a veracious observer records is a contribution, however small, to our general sum of knowledge.

It only remains to say that a few of these chapters have appeared in *Nature Notes* and in *The Girl's Own Paper.* The rest are now printed for the first time.

ELIZA BRIGHTWEN.

TABLE OF CONTENTS.

LIST OF ILLUSTRATIONS.

13

LEMURS.

"In consecrated earth
And on the holy hearth
The Lars and Lemurs moan with midnight plaint."

MILTON.

MONGST the many curious animals I had kept and studied, there had never, so far, been a specimen of the monkey tribe. I had always feared that I could not meet their requirements in the way of food and temperature, and that a proper place for such creatures did not exist at the Grove.

However, the offer of a pair of lemurs tempted me into many consultations and much searching

B 17

amongst the books in the library, in order to find
out all that could be learned about the nature of
these animals, until I found myself speculating as
to whether it would not, after all, be possible to
make them happy.

Lemurs are inhabitants of the island of Madagascar, where they live in the woods, feeding on
fruits. All accounts agree in describing them as
quiet, gentle creatures, very agile in their movements and nocturnal in their habits.

The word *lemur* was employed by the ancients
to describe the unbodied spirits of men, whether
beneficent or malignant; the festivals called
lemuria were appointed for the appeasing and
"laying" of ghosts. The animals received their
name from their almost noiseless movements;
they must, I suppose, look very ghastly and un-
canny as they flit about on the tree-branches at
night.

The more I read about them the more it
appeared to me that I must not lightly pass by
such an opportunity of obtaining rare subjects for
naturalistic study. So the lemurs were accepted,
and I sent a man to the other side of London

to bring them, cage and all, with great care to their new home.

Until I knew their size and something about their requirements I could not very well prepare a place for them, and I reckoned on their living in the cage that they came in for a few days at least after their arrival. What, then, was my dismay when the lemurs arrived to find that they were packed in a small hamper, and that no cage had come with them, as it had been found too large to be conveyed by any cab or other sort of carriage.

Plainly the poor animals could not stay in the hamper, and I had nothing large enough to hold them. They were so timid that I was afraid to let them loose in the conservatory; they might have sprung up to the roof and remained there, where it would be cold, and as I had been very specially warned to guard them against draughts, I was puzzled indeed to know what to do with them. At last a large circular linen-basket was found, which made a temporary home until we could think of some better place in which to keep them.

When the hamper was opened the poor frightened creatures were seen, locked in each other's
arms, gazing at us with round glassy eyes. It
was some days before we could really see what
beautiful animals they were, since their timidity
was so great that, though they would eat bananas
out of my hand gently enough, nothing would
induce them to come out of their hiding-place
and be friendly.

As soon as possible, a bay at one end of the
conservatory was wired in, some tree-branches
were fixed for the lemurs to climb upon, and a
large plant-case, with glass sides and top, and
soft hay within, made a cosy retreat when they
wished for complete retirement.

It was very enjoyable to let the new pets into
their pleasant home. They instantly and fully
approved of it, climbing at once to the highest
branch, and gazing down at us with a far happier
expression in their great eyes than they had
hitherto shown. And now for the first time we
could appreciate the beauty of their silky-white
fur and wonderful tails.

I found out that these were specimens of the

Ruffed Lemur, the most beautiful of the ten species found in Madagascar. I will try and describe them, though it will not be easy to give a very clear idea of creatures which vary so much in aspect according to the position they adopt.

Sitting on the top of their glass house, side by side, with their long furry tails coiled around them, they looked like two huge Persian cats, but standing or climbing they showed themselves to be true monkeys, although far exceeding the ordinary monkey in gracefulness.

Round the head was a full ruff of long white hairs, setting off the gentle, fox-like face, which was mostly black, as were the small, well-shaped hands and feet. Lemurs have four fingers and a thumb on the hands, and the great toe and four smaller ones, as well as the fingers, have perfect nails, which makes the creatures look very human.

The thick woolly fur was white, with large patches of black, and the tail, three-quarters of a yard in length, was precisely like a lady's black fur boa, and was used much in the same way, either laid gracefully across the back or over the feet, or wherever else warmth might be required.

When I offered food to these lemurs they had a curious way of obtaining it when not quite within their reach. The little black hand was stretched out and took a firm but very gentle grasp of my fingers, drawing them nearer until the coveted fruit could be reached, and even if the banana could have been taken direct they preferred to hold my hand, and did it so prettily that I was tempted always to make them reach out for it.

Considering the ghost-like character associated with these animals, we thought that "Spectre" and "Phantom" would be appropriate names; they do not, however, respond to any endearing epithets, and only manifest emotion when a banana is offered for their acceptance.

I fancy they are somewhat unintelligent; they differ greatly from the ordinary type of monkey, in that they sit still by the hour together, and have no idea of mischief or of helping themselves in any way; for instance, a monkey, if feeling cold, will accept a shawl and wrap it round him, finding the comfort of it; but these creatures would sit and shiver and die of cold before the idea of covering themselves would enter their dull brains.

They are masters of the art of expressing surprise and contempt. If something is offered to them that they do not like, they bridle up and turn away their heads as much as to say, "Dear me, no! nothing earthly would induce me to touch a thing like that ; remove it at once ! "

My greatest surprise in connection with the lemurs took place about two months after their arrival. I had carried Mungo[1] to see them, and carefully holding him by his string, I allowed him to stand and gaze up at them through the wires.

He had often done this before, and beyond a few angry snorts and their usual grunting sounds they had taken no notice, but on this occasion they both at the same moment set up the most terrific roar that I ever heard. I do not exaggerate when I declare that it really seemed as loud as the roar of a lion at the Zoo. I was close to them, and it was so utterly unexpected I don't think I was ever quite so astonished in all my life. The sound was truly awful, and it lasted for half a minute or more, till I felt completely stunned, and was glad

[1] My pet mongoose.

enough to retreat to a quiet room where my nerves could recover from the shock.

I think the Madagascar woods where these animals dwell must be most gruesome places at night, with these black and white creatures flitting about in the branches, abruptly uttering their terrific roars at intervals.

A family quarrel among lemurs must be a thing to remember. Besides this, they also give a loud groan now and then, which irresistibly reminds one of *Punch's* "moaning gipsy in the back garden." Such a groan must sound additionally weird at night in the dark woods.

When I gave my friends an account of the scare I had had, one of them returned with me to the conservatory to be favoured with a special performance of "Ghosts." Mungo was brought in once more, and up rose the awful sound, with such effect that my friend turned and fled, even though she had been forewarned. Fear is quite irresistibly awakened by the strange quality of the sound given forth by these animals. Having very slight means of defending themselves, I imagine this roaring power has been bestowed upon them to enable them to scare their foes, and drive away through fear such enemies as their soft hands could never overcome in fair fight.

After keeping these lemurs about a year, I found that by no amount of kindness or coaxing could I get them to be really friendly, and I feared they were not over-happy without companions of their own kind. They were doubtless caught too old to be tamed. It was therefore deemed best to present them to the Zoo, where, under the kind and skilful treatment they receive, they are, I believe, in splendid health and spirits.

Visitors to the monkey-house can identify them from the description I have here given, and cannot fail to admire the agile movements and furry beauty of my quondam pets.

TOMMY AND PEARLIE.

"So abundant, indeed, are lemurs in Madagascar, that, according to M. Grandidier, who has done so much to increase our knowledge of this group, at least one individual is almost sure to be found in every little copse throughout the island."

TOMMY AND PEARLIE.

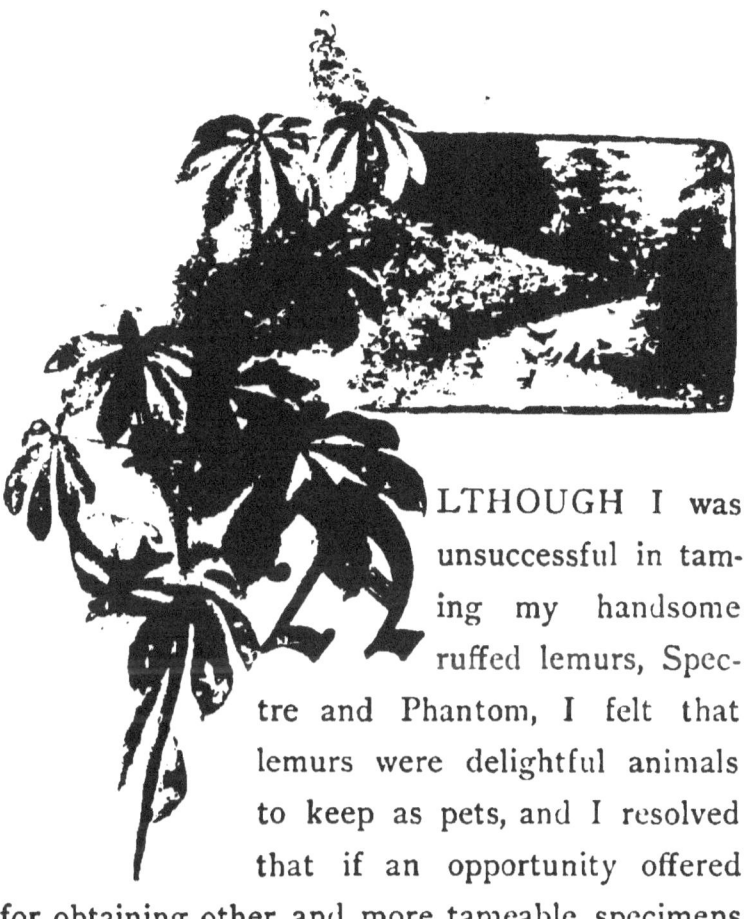

LTHOUGH I was unsuccessful in taming my handsome ruffed lemurs, Spectre and Phantom, I felt that lemurs were delightful animals to keep as pets, and I resolved that if an opportunity offered for obtaining other and more tameable specimens of the same kind I would certainly try again, and with my past experience I hoped to attain good results.

One day I heard that a young specimen of a
Ruffed Lemur had been seen in a cage at the top
of a cart full of birds and curious animals, a sort of
small travelling menagerie which was stopping for
a few days at a town five miles off. A mounted
messenger was sent off at once with a basket, and
full directions about the purchase of the little
lemur, and, to my great delight, when the man
returned with it, it proved to be all I could desire,
quite young and healthy and very tame.

It must have been a pleasant change from the
cold, draughty cage it had been used to, to the
large wired-in recess in my conservatory, which
was always kept at a genial temperature, and
where, leaping from branch to branch, the agile
little creature could play its graceful frolics from
morning till night, hanging head downwards,
swinging on a trapeze like a born acrobat, and
evidently enjoying its life as much as if it had been
in its native woods. The showman had always
called the lemur Tommy, so we supposed that was
an indication of its sex, and retained the name
to which it had been accustomed.

One day in summer I had one of my large

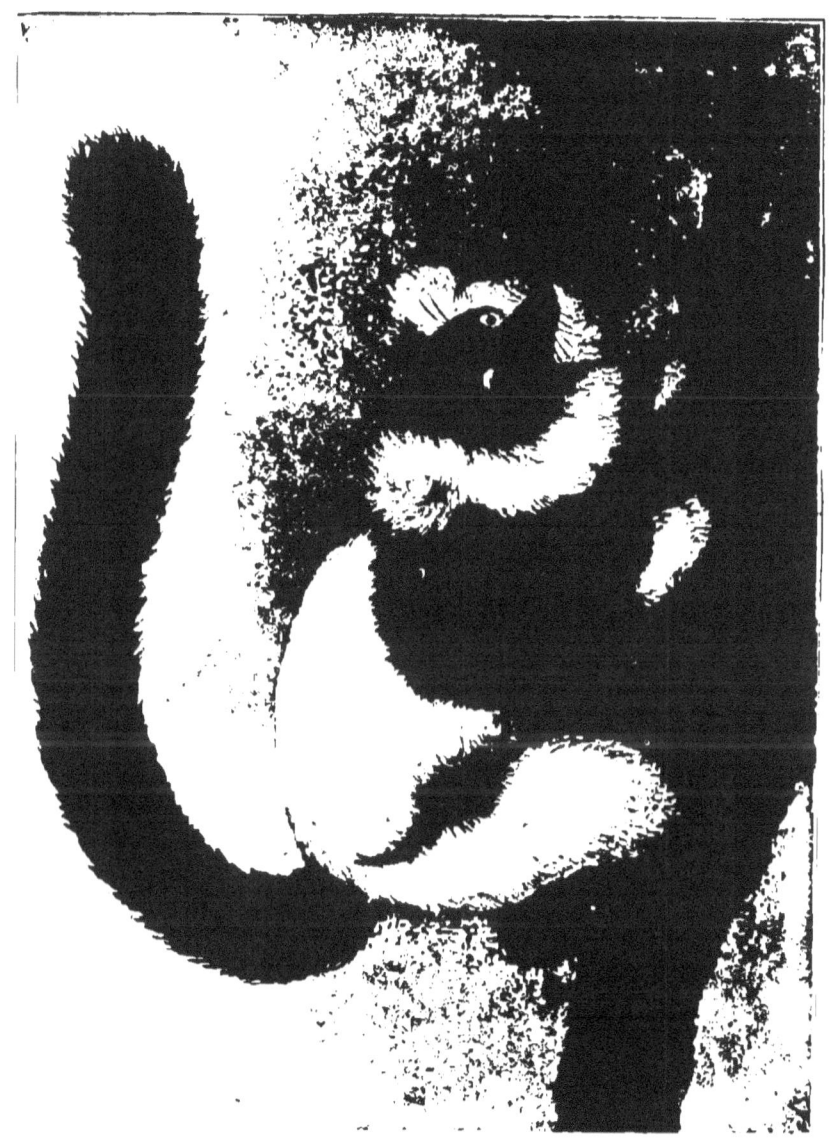

TOMMY.

parties of poor people in the garden, and Tommy was led about with a long string, greatly to the delight of my visitors. The lemur was in no way frightened by the crowd; he made friends with everybody, and hopped about from one group to another quite at his ease. After a time a harp and violin began to sound, and then Tommy's love of music became apparent, for he seated himself close to the players, and there he remained quite riveted by the unusual sounds, gazing intently at the harpist as if spellbound.

They were but village musicians, and I was not a little surprised when, on my remarking how music was appreciated by the lemur, one of the men remarked, "It keeps reminding me of King Robert of Sicily and his 'solemn ape.'" One hardly expected such a knowledge of Longfellow's poetry in a country rustic !

It is not the first time I have been scared by the display of unlooked-for intelligence, as the following anecdote will show.

Many years ago I was talking to my cook on culinary matters in the dining-room, when she suddenly looked up at a majolica plate over the doorway, and said, " That's a mythological subject isn't it, ma'am?" I replied that it was. She then said, "Is that Pan in the foreground?" I said, " No, but it is a Satyr." "Well," replied Cookie, " I was saying the other day to the butler, if there were creatures of that sort to be seen nowadays it would go far to prove the Darwinian theory — wouldn't it, ma'am?" History does not record my reply! I gazed at the creature depicted on the plate, half man and half animal, and felt there was much acumen in my learned servant's remark, but, the question of that day's dinner being once settled, I thought it best to leave the Darwinian theory alone, lest I might not prove equal to the occasion.

This, however, is a digression. I have now to record the advent of Tommy's companion, Pearlie. It seemed well that the lemur should have a play- mate, and I often endeavoured to provide one, but· was unsuccessful, until one day, on visiting the Bedford Conservatories in Covent Garden, I saw some pretty grey creature curled up in a cage, and on inquiry I found that it was a specimen of another species, the Ring-Tailed Lemur, quite young and very tame. It was just what I wanted,

c

so the little animal was carefully packed in a hamper, and I brought it home with me.

I feared to place this little lemur at once with Tommy, lest they might not agree, so, for the night, the new pet was placed in a large basket, and covered with a railway rug. Next morning it was discovered on the top of the highest picture frame, having forced its way out of the basket. A banana soon tempted it to come down, and in the most friendly manner it sat upon my shoulder and seemed delighted to be caressed and played with. Before long, when the two lemurs had become accustomed to each other, they were allowed to meet, and quickly became the greatest friends, playing together for hours and affording us constant amusement in watching their graceful gambols.

These lemurs are always giving me surprises. I was quite unprepared for the remarkable power the ring-tailed lemur possesses of running swiftly up the flat surface of a door, but this Pearlie did with the greatest ease, and then sat calmly looking down at me from the top as if enjoying my amazement. I was led to examine his paws, and found

PEARLIE BASKING BEFORE THE FIRE.

they were provided with elastic pads somewhat like a fly's foot with its suckers, and then reading about this particular species I learned that it inhabits a rocky tableland without trees, so that it is not arboreal in its habits, but is formed with leather-like palms to its hands to enable it to keep a firm footing on wet and slippery rocks, where it is not possible for human beings, although barefooted, to follow it. When he is brought into a sitting-room it is very needful to have a leading-string attached to Pearlie's waistband, else he darts away and is at the top of a picture frame out of reach in a moment. His agility is only second to that of the Gibbon — the wonderful spider-like monkey one may sometimes see at the Zoological Gardens performing marvels of agility in swinging, by means of his attenuated arms and legs.

During the summer months my lemurs much enjoy being in the open air, and on fine days they are tethered on the lawn, where they amuse my visitors with their graceful frolics. The entire absence of odour, their cleanly habits, and their delicate tastes as to diet render these animals especially desirable as pets ; they enjoy fruit of all kinds — lettuces, clover-blossoms, and rose-petals, while dates, raisins, and bread and milk supply solid items of food. Thus fed and warmly housed these creatures can be kept in splendid health with very little trouble.

Pearlie was so named from his fur being of a soft pearl-grey colour, the long tail being banded with alternate rings of black and white. His face and chest are also curiously marked in black and white, the eyes bright orange, and the general expression is as gentle as that of a little cat.

We found out in the course of time that Tommy was of the gentler sex! Her name must therefore be considered the diminutive for Thomasina — at least I see no other way out of the difficulty, as a new name would not be responded to or understood.

Pearlie's portrait requires a word of explanation. His great delight in cold weather is to be allowed to sit on a hassock before the drawing-room fire and bask in its warmth. The instant he is seated before the cheerful blaze, up go his little arms in a worshipping attitude like a veritable Parsee. Thus he will remain for hours content and happy as long as I am in the room, but if left alone he makes a pitiful cry and starts off in search of some of his friends, as though life were not endurable without human companionship. I think this is always the case where animals are treated with uniform kindness ; they must be able to trust those who feed and care for them, and when that perfect trust is established they yield a love that is often quite touching in its intensity. These two lemurs are very different in character. Tommy is absolutely selfish and strongly self-willed, timid and cautious. Pearlie shines by contrast, and is ready to give up, gentle, affectionate, and confiding. It is true they are of different species, and that may in a measure account for the differing characters they exhibit, but seeing they were both obtained when quite young, and treated alike with unvarying kindness, one would have thought that original tendencies would have become more thoroughly effaced. Allowing for Tommy's moral failings, one must own that he and Pearlie are delightful specimens of the monkey tribe. They keep their lovely fur spotlessly clean, are quite inodorous, always ready to be caressed, and add greatly to the interest of my conservatory by their lively movements and graceful antics.

MUNGO.

MUNGO.

UNGO, the Ichneumon, whose early life was chronicled in "More about Wild Nature," has now been a household pet for nearly four years, and must be nearly six years old.

I do not know how long these animals generally live, but as yet Mungo shows no signs of age or infirmity. He is as full of fun and as inquisitive as ever, but not so bent upon mischief as in his youthful days. He now has the range of house and garden, and goes wherever he likes without even a collar to remind him of captivity.

The chief trouble is in connection with my visitors — those at least who have a strong objection to "wild animals about the house"; nothing, however, can possibly be less "wild" than Mungo, for he is just like a tame cat. He does not dream of biting or scratching, and is never so happy as when curled up in the lap of some indulgent friend; yet, as he unfortunately looks like a ferret, many people find it very hard to believe that he can be perfectly harmless.

Mungo delights to spend his mornings basking in the sun on the window-sill of my bedroom, where he is sufficiently elevated to watch all that goes on in the garden. He is scarcely ever asleep; as Mr. Rudyard Kipling says so truly, in the delightful account he gives of an Indian Mongoose in the *Jungle Book*, "He is eaten up from nose to tail with curiosity," and whilst seeming to slumber, the active little cinnamon-coloured nose is ever on the work sniffing out the varied movements of the household.

As summer comes on we naturally let the fire die out ; and Mungo strongly disapproves of this custom, for he dearly loves to bask on a little wool mat before a hot fire. Now, however, he adopts another plan — when he finds the fire is out he quietly climbs over the wire-guard, goes under the grate and there lies down amongst the warm ashes. He has even done this whilst there remained some fire in the grate, and I much fear he may make an *auto-da-fe* of himself some day by setting his long hair alight, which would be a terrible fate indeed for our cherished pet.

Mungo's love of warmth leads to another undesirable habit. He will steal into the bedrooms and hide himself under the duvets, and — low be it spoken !— he has been found cosily rolled up in a nightdress !

It may naturally be asked, "Why is he not kept in a suitable wired-in place where he can do no harm ?" Simply because he makes himself perfectly miserable in confinement ; he tears at the wirework till his paws are bleeding, and foams at the mouth with misery and rage. No one could keep an amiable little animal in such purgatory; it would be kinder to end its life at once, and such a fate cannot even be thought of.

Mungo is a diplomatist! Liberty he has schemed to obtain, and after years of astute planning, and almost reasoning, he has reached his end, and we must acknowledge ourselves beaten, for to all intents and purposes he is now master of the situation and may do pretty much what he pleases.

There is, however, still a crumpled roseleaf in his lot; the softest bed and the sunniest nook to bask in will not satisfy Mungo without human society, and as we cannot give up all other occupations in order to sit with him, he is often to be seen wandering about like an unquiet spirit until he finds some friendly lap where he can curl himself up and enjoy all those conditions of warmth, ease, and society which form his idea of perfect bliss.

I am sure Mungo is a staunch Conservative as to his political views! He hates changes of any kind, since they interfere with his personal comfort and methodical habits. He likes to have a morning sleep in a sunny spot, and then his profound interest in a certain rhododendron bed, where rabbit-holes and mole-tracks are to be found, leads him to steal across the lawn and disappear amongst the bushes. I rather fancy he has grand times there, for if I attempt to coax him to come with me, his pert little nose will appear amidst the leaves, and with a frisk and a leap of absolute disobedience and fun he will return to his playground and remain there till it pleases him to come indoors again. His next desire is to enjoy a quiet afternoon under a warm duvet, and as he behaves with absolute propriety and only covets warmth and quietness, I am indulgent enough to allow him the luxury of being in my room until evening, when he is fed, wrapped up in a wool mat and a piece of baize and placed safely in his cage for the night.

Although Mungo would often absent himself for hours at a time, we were so sure to see him trotting quietly home when his frolics were ended, that somehow the possibility of an accident happening to him never crossed our minds. When, however, one day he did not return by evening, and night

came on and no one had seen or heard anything
of my pet, I felt certain he had met with some
sad fate — most probably had been caught in a
snare or trap set by the poachers on the common.
Next day, gardeners and farm-men were sent out
in all directions to look for him. The search
went on for many hours, and at last I heard
the welcome cry, "Mungo is found!" Poor
little fellow! but how my heart ached to see
him in torturing pain with a wild, scared look
in his eyes. He had, as we suspected, strayed
across the boundary on to the common, and
there he had been caught in a spring-trap, which
had completely crushed one of his fore-paws.

I had only a few minutes in which to decide
whether the poor little animal must be put out
of his misery at once or if there might be hope,
by skilful amputation, of ultimate recovery. I
am sure that all lovers of animals will understand
the keen distress I felt at having to make such a
decision, but something must be done, and as I
found I *could not* give the death warrant, Mungo
was taken to the veterinary doctor, with injunc-
tions to spare no pains in trying to save the patient

all needless suffering. Two surgeons attended to the case, and whilst under chloroform the little animal was relieved of the injured paw, and must have been remarkably well treated, for I was soon informed that Mungo was doing well and would take some "bird" for his dinner! In about a fortnight he was brought home and looked very pitiful, limping about on three legs. It was long before I could become accustomed to see him thus, but so well did the wound heal that now the limp can hardly be observed, and the little creature is as merry as ever, scampering about and playing with his own tail as lively as any kitten.

It has been an interest to me to make a study of the character of my mongoose, for a wild creature rendered perfectly tame by unvarying kind treatment gives one an excellent opportunity of observing the real nature of the animal.

I fear I must own that Mungo is absolutely selfish, his one idea is to enjoy perfect liberty and have his own way in everything. After four years' petting he knows me well as his friend and purveyor, but he has not an atom of affection;

he has, apparently, no mode of manifesting regard, the expression of his face never alters, he
does not try to lick my hand or make any greet-
ing sound. He likes to jump into my lap simply
because it is a comfortable place, and, as he
is very timid at any unwonted noise, he will run
to me for protection, but I am afraid he views
me as a means of attaining physical comfort,
food, and warmth, and nothing more!

All this does not prevent my liking the curious
little animal, but one cannot but be struck by the
immense difference between its nature and that
of the faithful dog, whose devotion to his master
will lead him to refuse his food, to take long,
toilsome journeys, to wait patiently for weary
hours in cold wind and biting frost when bidden
to guard his owner's flock, aye, and even to yield
up his life, if necessary, to do his master service.

All this shows, what I have often remarked
before, that, to those who are observant of the
fact, there is as much difference between the
characters of various animals, and even between
those of individuals of the same species, as may
be found in human beings.

Possibly Mungo may be a selfish specimen of his race, and there may exist brilliant exceptions abounding in affection and other noble qualities. I can only describe him as he is, and, judging by his small cranium and its peculiarly flattened formation, I should imagine he is formed to be, not a pattern of all the virtues, but a creature of one idea, and that — snake-killing! To be proficient in that art all the characteristics I have noted in this animal are specially needed, such as lynx-like watchfulness, undaunted courage in fight, persistent curiosity and determination to care for himself under all circumstances.

We must therefore wink at his failure in moral goodness, and admire the way in which he carries out the purpose for which he was made. He worthily adorns his own special niche in Creation.

D

SQUIRRELS WON BY KINDNESS.

" Drawn from his refuge in some lonely elm,
That age or injury has hollowed deep,
Where, on his bed of wool and matted leaves
He has outslept the winter, ventures forth
To frisk awhile, and bask in the warm sun,
The squirrel, flippant, pert, and full of play :
He sees me, and at once, swift as a bird,
Ascends the neighbouring beech ; there whisks his brush,
And perks his ears, and stamps and scolds aloud."

COWPER.

SQUIRRELS WON BY KINDNESS.

BOUT ten years ago we began taming the wild squirrels which exist in great numbers in the woods around this house. We put Barcelona nuts in a small basket outside the dining-room window, and every day a handful thrown on the ground served to attract the notice of the little animals. In a very short time the squirrels ventured to approach, timidly at first, picking up their favourite food ; they would scratch up the nuts and rush away to some quiet spot out of sight.

Generations of the graceful little rodents have been trained to come nearer and nearer to the window, until they are now so delightfully tame that I feel induced to suggest to others the means of enjoying the pleasure we find in watching our daily visitors from the woods.

My first act before breakfast is to place a handful of nuts on a small table which stands in the room close to a bay window. Hardly have I done so when in come the squirrels, sliding up to the window and leaping on to the table to enjoy the nuts. They will take nuts gently from our hands, and sitting up in the graceful position a squirrel adopts when quite at ease — its tail curved over its back, and its tiny paws holding the nut — they crack them and fling away the shells in careless fashion. A scrimmage sometimes takes place when several come in together ; one bolder spirit will chase another round the room until both spring out at the window and dart across the lawn. At length the nuts on the table being eaten or carried away, the squirrels, well knowing where the supply is kept, descend to the floor and hop leisurely to a cupboard, where on the first shelf is a box full of Barcelonas. The little animals spring on to the shelf and help themselves. This they are allowed to do for a little while, as we like to watch their proceedings; but I make a protest presently, and close the cupboard door when I find my entire stock of nuts being transferred to the garden and planted all over the lawn, for the squirrels bury nuts for future use, although I am very doubtful whether they do really dig them up again.

On cold mornings when the windows cannot be opened, it is touching to see the little furry heads peep through the pane, waiting patiently for their daily meal. This they eventually share with several very tame nuthatches; these birds seeming very glad of nuts as well as fat during the winter months.

The only drawback to having wild squirrels tamed is the distraction they cause when a class of village children is being taught in the dining-room ! Sydney Smith says : " A sparrow fluttering about the church is an antagonist which the most pro-found theologian in Europe is wholly unable to overcome," and certainly the apparition of a bright-eyed squirrel popping up at each window in succession is enough to drive a teacher to despair. Nothing less than an abundant shower of nuts will bribe the little intruders to keep quiet for a time.

I have given these simple details because I think that possibly many of my readers may like to encourage those charming little animals when they learn how easily, by a little patient kindness, they may be attracted from the woods to become household pets of their own free will, which is, to my mind, so much more enjoyable than keeping captive animals or birds. It should, perhaps, be added that great quietness and calm are needed while the first advances are being made, and that a loud voice or a quick gesture will undo a week's work in taming.

A "FAIRY" STORY.

"I joyed to hear her own peculiar note
    Through all the music float;
But when the gentle song, that streamed away,
Like some enamoured rivulet that flows
Under a night of leaves and flowering may,
Died on the stress of its own lovely pain,
    Even as it died away,
It seemed as if no influence could restrain
The notes from welling in the whitethroat's brain."

EDMUND GOSSE.

I AM often envied as the possessor of one of the most charming bird-pets it is possible to imagine.

"Fairy" is a tiny white-throat, a sleek, delicate, grey-coloured bird, with a white breast, lovely in form, swift in flight, and of most engaging disposition.

I met with it in this wise. A plaintive little cheeping sound attracted my attention one morning at breakfast-time, and looking outside the window, I saw a tiny, half-fledged bird sitting on the ground, looking pitifully up at me; it pleaded its hungry condition with open beak, and seemed to have no fear at my approach. Of course such a poor little motherless waif must be cared for, so I brought it in, and it received very readily the provender I offered it.

I never saw such a tiny, quaint-looking piece of bird-life. Its little throat-feathers were beginning to show on either side like a small white cravat; it had about half an inch of tail, and minute quills all over its body gave token of coming feathers. The delightful thing about it was its exceeding tameness; it would sit on my finger and gaze at me with a contemplative expression; no noise frightened it; it was quite content with life in a basket, or on the table, and therefore it became my constant companion, and has grown to be very dear to me and to a wide circle of friends.

Fairy's advent was in July, and for the first month the early morning feeding was no small care; but love makes all things easy, and at last my small charge could feed itself, and had learnt the use of its wings.

Daily baths were taken in my soap-dish, which

was amply large enough at first, but now Fairy is promoted to the sponge basin, in which she flutters to her heart's content and dries herself afterwards by swift flights about the room. The bath over, the next thing is to search for flies on the window-panes or on the floor; these are snapped up as great dainties, and in this way Fairy greatly promoted my comfort all through the heat of August and September, 1893, by keeping my room free of winged insects.

I have only to take Fairy on my finger and direct her attention to a fly on the ceiling, when off she darts, like a hawk after its quarry, and the fly disappears like magic.

I was once much amused to watch her day after day eyeing a large spider in the corner of the room. She evidently considered very deeply whether she could tackle it; it was large and she was small, and for three days she hesitated; but at last her courage was equal to the enterprise, and the spider was seized, minced up, and eaten. My tiny pet lives on grapes, lettuce, flies, meal-worms, and, as great indulgences, cream and sugar; a tin of special bird-food supplies other items of diet.

Fairy is in and out of her cage all day, and but for fear of accidents she might have the range of the house, so confident am I that she would not wish to stray from her happy home. Still, she loves an expedition, and once, having flown after me into the hall, I did not see her again for an hour or more; a hunt was needful, and after searching every room she was at last discovered cheerfully investigating the boxes in a lumber-room at the very top of the house.

I never knew such a clever, fearless little bird. She will put her small body into every corner in search of information; she visits all my friends in turn as they sit at luncheon, pulls their hair, sits on their fingers, tugs their dresses, and is, of course, universally beloved.

I was curious to note whether Fairy would grow restless when the migrating season began, but her abnormal life indoors has so altered her natural instincts that she makes herself quite happy throughout the autumn, and we are truly glad that we are not called to bid adieu to such a lovable companion.

Very naturally some readers may ask, "How

can they obtain a tame, happy little pet bird such as my whitethroat now is?" I can only reply, such a thing is not to be bought (or very rarely) for any amount of money, but can be attained by any one who will bring up a young fledgling from its earliest youth, with never-failing love and gentleness. There is no secret about it; it is not a gift bestowed on some and withheld from others, as many seem to suppose, judging from the number of times I have been told, "Oh, you have the gift of taming creatures." I always disclaim the assertion and tell the simple truth, that just as you seek to win the heart of a child by invariable and patient kindness, so these innocent dumb brethren of ours yield us their devoted love if they meet with similar treatment at our hands.

We must not begin the task of bringing up a young bird without counting the cost beforehand. It means rising every morning between four and five, and having little sleep afterwards, for we must imitate the self-denying industry of the mother-bird in providing food for her young ones. If we look out over the dewy lawns at daybreak

in spring and summer, we shall see thrushes,
blackbirds, robins, and many other birds all
actively engaged in searching for worms and
insects to supply the needs of their respective
families. All through the day we must think of
the tender creature we have undertaken to rear,
giving it every half-hour as much food as it
desires, and keeping it warmly covered from
cold and draughts, lest its limbs should be
attacked by cramp.

This ailment seems incurable, and is the cruel
fate of most fledglings that are brought away from
their parents, because people forget that the
warmth of the mother-bird is essential to the life
of the callow brood, and I, for one, never promote
the rearing of young wild birds unless, as in the
case of a motherless waif like my Fairy, we try
to save a little innocent life by doing what we can
to imitate its natural bringing up. Absolute tameness can only be attained by unvarying gentle
treatment. Never has Fairy heard a harsh word, or,
as far as I know, has she had a fright of any kind.

A single grip of Mungo's cruel little jaws would
end her life in a moment, but Fairy does not know

FAIRY SINGING.

E

it, and she sings on fearlessly as he passes her
cage. I believe she would act as a certain much-
petted little dog used to do when his mistress pre-
tended to scold him severely ; he would look about
eagerly to see where the wicked animal addressed
could be that he might fly at him. I tried
to speak seriously to my small bird one day
when she was particularly in my way, but she
only gave me several hard pecks, and to my
great amusement fought me with her tiny claws
much as a gamecock would use his spurs. Fairy
has the curious habit, which I have noticed in
many small birds, of turning rapid somersaults
by way of exercise, springing from a perch
on one side of the cage up to the roof, turning
over and coming down on her feet like a born
acrobat.

It is curious to be able to see human passions
manifested in such a tiny creature as my whitethroat, and it can rarely *be seen*, because it is
very seldom that a bird is so absolutely tame as
to feel free to show itself as it is in reality —
fear being the dominant feeling in most captive
birds — and that leads to the incessant fluttering

and effort to escape, which hinders character from being shown.

When Fairy is out of her cage, if I open a drawer she is certain to show *curiosity*, and flies into it, hops about in her perky way, pecking at one thing and another to find out what each is, her beak being equivalent to a hand, and the only instrument with which she can do anything. I put some delicacy on my finger, and then she comes, and by her actions and low chirping she shows *pleasure*.

Before long, her sweet warbling song expresses *contentment*, her little sky is serene and clear, all her wants are provided for, she has no cares for the morrow, and her happy little nature comes out in cheery songs.

She picks a scarlet flower petal, and I am not sure but it may be poisonous and bad for her, so, like a careful mother, I take it out of her beak. Then comes unmistakable *anger;* she scolds and pecks at my fingers, and wilfully tries to get the flower petal back again.

All this is wonderfully human, and all to be found in a creature not two inches in length!

If Fairy could be seen minus her feathers she would be about the size of a walnut! I do think in all respects a *bird* is one of the principal marvels of creation, most lovely and lovable. See the little creature taking a bath, reducing itself to a disreputable tuft of draggled feathers for the sake of cleanliness, and then fluttering and shaking itself dry again, and by means of its wonderful beak pluming its feathers into order, applying oil to them from its little gland just above the tail, and after infinite pains ending by looking soft and sleek as a piece of satin.

Instinct teaches it to do all this which we could no more imitate than we could fly. Then how touching is the motherhood of a bird. Many a human mother is put to shame by the example of a little feathered thing which has only instinct to guide her in preparing her soft, warm nursery, to which love ties her closely for two or three weeks. Bright days come and go, but she denies herself all the pleasures she sees other birds enjoying, and barely takes time to get her needful food, that she may keep warm those two little snowy eggs which are all the world to her even now, and when young creatures begin to stir beneath her faithful breast then she exchanges the quiescent life for one of incessant toil that her callow brood may not call to her in vain for the insect diet which she has to provide.

By the time the young ones can feed themselves the parents are quite thin and worn with their incessant toil, and yet in favourable seasons some kinds of birds rear a second or even a third family before the summer is over.

Although the Whitethroat is plentiful in the southern counties, I do not find that people, as a rule, are at all familiar with its appearance, and I imagine this arises from the shy habits of the bird. It flits nimbly out of sight when alarmed, and being of an inconspicuous grey colour, it requires a keen eye to distinguish it when hopping noiselessly about in weedy hedgerows, where it is so often found that it has obtained the provincial name of Nettle Creeper.

With reference to the migration of the Whitethroat, I learn from one of Canon Tristram's delightful books on birds, that Algeria is its winter retreat. He says : —

"Each portion of the Sahara — the rocky ridges, the sand drifts, the plains — has its peculiar ornithological characteristics. But by far the most interesting localities are, as might have been anticipated, the dayats and the oases. Here are the winter quarters of many of our familiar summer visitants. The chiff-chaff, willow-wren, and whitethroat hop on every twig in the gardens shadowed by the never-failing palm; the swallow and the window martin thread the lanes and sport over the mouths of the wells in pursuit of the swarming mosquitoes."

When spring returns, these smaller birds are led by instinct to re-cross the Mediterranean and seek their European haunts where the temperature has again become sufficiently mild to enable them to find insect food and rear their families of nestlings.

The sharp clicking note, like two stones jarred together, which this bird makes when excited, we constantly hear in our furze-bushes and hedges, proving that the Whitethroat exists in some numbers in Middlesex; and now that my "Fairy" has begun to sing, I find it is a strain with which I am quite familiar. My curiosity had often been excited by hearing low, soft warbles from unseen singers on the common or in the woods; I vainly tried to see what bird it could be, but it always seemed to remain out of sight. My small pet has solved the mystery by performing for my private benefit the sweet music of her wild brethren out of doors.

I am constantly reminded of the lines in Coleridge's "Ancient Mariner" : —

> " A noise like of a hidden brook
> In the leafy month of June,
> That to the sleeping wood all night
> Singeth a quiet tune."

As I sit at my writing, the delicate soft warbling goes on hour after hour, and is a source of real pleasure to me, so manifestly is it the outcome of a perfectly happy little spirit telling out its inward joy in its own sweet fashion.

Captivity has no terrors for Fairy; she loves her cage, and will hardly leave it except when she occasionally takes a swift flight to and fro, and then alights on my notepaper to give a peck at my pen. She delights in sitting on the fender, fluffing up her feathers to revel in the warmth, which, in winter, is her substitute for sunshine, and before long she returns to her own little home, where she may be seen gracefully sipping the sweet juice of a grape before recommencing her song.

I often wonder how long this, my latest pet, may be spared to me! A bird's life is such a tender thing — a moment's carelessness may rob one of a cherished pet, and the greatest care will not always guard such a tiny swift-flying bird from injury.

May the sorrowful day be far distant that shall see me bereft of my little ray of home sunshine, my Fairy Whitethroat!

ASNAPPER.

" Heard ye the Owl
Hoot to her mate responsive? 'Twas not she
Whom, floating on white pinions near his barn,
The farmer views well-pleased, and bids his boy
Forbear her nest; but she who, cloth'd in robe
Of unobtrusive brown, regardless flies
Mouse-haunted corn-stacks and the thresher's floor,
And prowls for plunder in the lonely wood."

ASNAPPER.

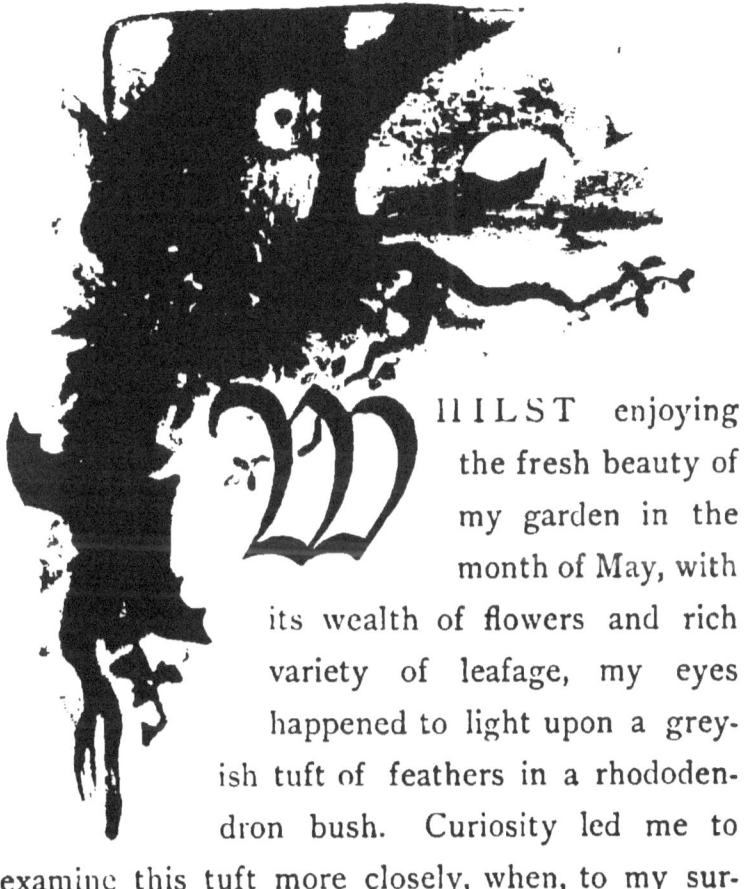

HILST enjoying
the fresh beauty of
my garden in the
month of May, with
its wealth of flowers and rich
variety of leafage, my eyes
happened to light upon a greyish tuft of feathers in a rhododendron bush. Curiosity led me to
examine this tuft more closely, when, to my surprise, I found it was a young brown owl—alive, but

in a very exhausted condition. It appeared to be
only a few weeks old, fully feathered, but unable
to feed itself; I suppose it had fallen out of the
nest and was dying for lack of food. I need
hardly say I carried it indoors, and did my best to
feed and restore the poor orphan, and right well
did he second my efforts. A juicy uncooked
mutton chop was cut up and mixed with feathers,
and with resounding snaps of his great beak the
morsels were received and swallowed. A second
chop was disposed of before my friend seemed
satisfied, and with such a mighty appetite I felt
there would be no difficulty in rearing this vigor-
ous infant. Next morning I found two sparrows
and a mouse had been obtained. These soon disappeared, and had to be supplemented by a piece
of raw meat. And if this is the daily diet of a
very young owl, we may form some idea of the way
in which full-grown birds must reduce the hordes
of mice and rats which would otherwise overrun
the country.

Whenever we passed the owl's cage he gave a
resounding snap with his beak, not viciously but
as a friendly recognition, and somehow this habit

suggested the name of the Assyrian king, the "noble Asnapper," and this, familiarly contracted to "Snap" for every-day use, became the recognised title of our new pet.

Asnapper lived quietly enough during the day in a large cage well covered from the light, but towards evening, when he had enjoyed his second repast of raw meat, he began to wake up and long for exercise. He was allowed his liberty in the house, and made full use of this privilege by going about from room to room, either running along the floor like a grey rabbit, or taking short flights with his noiseless wings. He would gravely pursue his way up the stairs a step at a time, and seemed to enjoy watching cattle in the fields whilst sitting motionless on a window-sill.

Until the bird could feed himself it would have been no kindness to let him go out of doors and starve, so I resolved to make the creature's life as happy as possible, whilst I had thus a good opportunity of learning the habits of an interesting species of bird. I could not help being somewhat afraid of his formidable curved beak, which looked as if it could inflict a severe wound, but I soon learned how gently Asnapper could use it; he would play with my fingers and hold them with such care that we had merry games of play at evening recreation time, when he looked to be let out of his cage and go where he pleased for an hour or two.

If allowed to be in the drawing-room the sociable bird made himself quite one of the party. Perched on the back of a chair, he would watch all that went on with a grave air of consideration, or else he would amuse himself by chasing a ball, or cotton reel, upon the floor, as if trying to make believe it was a mouse. I could not have thought there was so much latent fun in a solemn-looking owl, but then we are never out at night perched up in the tree-branches to see what goes on there amongst young owlets, so this afforded us a rather unusual glimpse into the habits and manners of the bird of wisdom in his merry days of youth.

This species, called the brown or tawny owl (*Syrnium stridula*), is found in most of the counties of England; it is rare in Scotland, and has not, I believe, been met with in Ireland. It generally retires to thick woods during the day, coming out at night to feed upon rabbits, moles, rats, mice, frogs, and insects.

When Asnapper had more food than he could consume at one meal he would hide the rest, taking pains to secrete his choice morsels in some dark

YOUNG BROWN OWL (ASNAPPER).

corner where he thought we could not see them. His soft blue eyes used to look very roguish as he peered round to see if we were watching him; those eyes, by the way, changed to a rich dark brown as he grew older, and would be, I fancy, quite black when full grown.

I have several times observed a brown owl flying quite late in the evening closely pursued by
enraged blackbirds screaming their loudest notes
of anger and fear, and I gather from this that the
owl is apt to prey upon small birds and possibly
robs their nests of eggs or young fledglings.

Several writers assert that this bird also feeds
on fish, being able to catch those swimming near
the surface. There can be no doubt of the
extreme value of owls in reducing the number
of rats and mice, and it is to be hoped that
landowners, in their own interest, if for no better
motive, will take pains to instruct their game-
keepers to protect such useful allies to the farmer
and gardener. I met with an amusing instance
of the value of the owl as a mouser when staying
at a farmhouse in Surrey. The farmer's daughter
told me her brother had just discovered "a
'howl's' nest in the pigeon coo," and going up a
ladder to examine it more closely had found two
eggs in the nest, and ranged around it were fourteen dead mice! If that was the result of one
evening's foraging, we need no other proof that
owls are worthy of encouragement and protection.

This anecdote relates to a barn owl, which may well be called the "farmer's friend," for it delights to roost in barns and outbuildings, where it can find plenty of mice, its favourite food, and on that account it should meet with a kind welcome instead of being trapped and shot and hung up to decorate the end of some outhouse, where I often grieve to see it, in company with the equally useful little kestrel and other hawks.

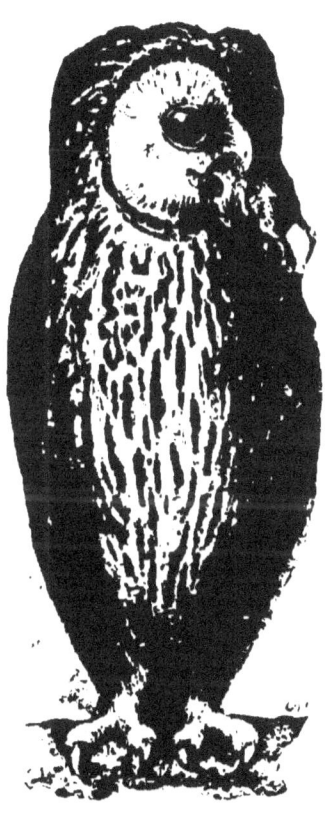

The brown owl has very different tastes as to its home, preferring a hollow tree in some secluded wood far away

ASNAPPER.

from human dwellings, although, from Mr. Waterton's experience, it will sometimes fly into houses in the dusk of evening. He says: "This pretty aërial wanderer of the night often comes into

F

my room, and after flitting to and fro on wing so soft and silent that he is scarcely heard, he takes his departure from the same window at which he entered." Mr. Waterton suggests that these birds may be encouraged to settle in our woods; if holes are made in pollard-trees that are slightly decayed, the brown owls will readily adopt them as nesting-places.

I have not as yet heard Asnapper make any sound except the characteristic snap of his beak, and a low whining cry of eager pleasure at sight of his accustomed food. We are very familiar with the loud, melancholy hoot of his kith and kin which we frequently hear at intervals during the night in the gardens and woods around the house, and Asnapper will join in the chorus, for, as soon as he can feed himself, we shall bid him an affectionate farewell, and have the pleasure of seeing him spread his broad wings and sail away to his native woods.

WILLOW-WRENS.

" The least and last of things
That soar on quivering wings,
Or crawl among the grass-blades out of sight
Have just as clear a right
To their appointed portion of delight
As Queens or Kings."

CHRISTINA ROSSETTI.

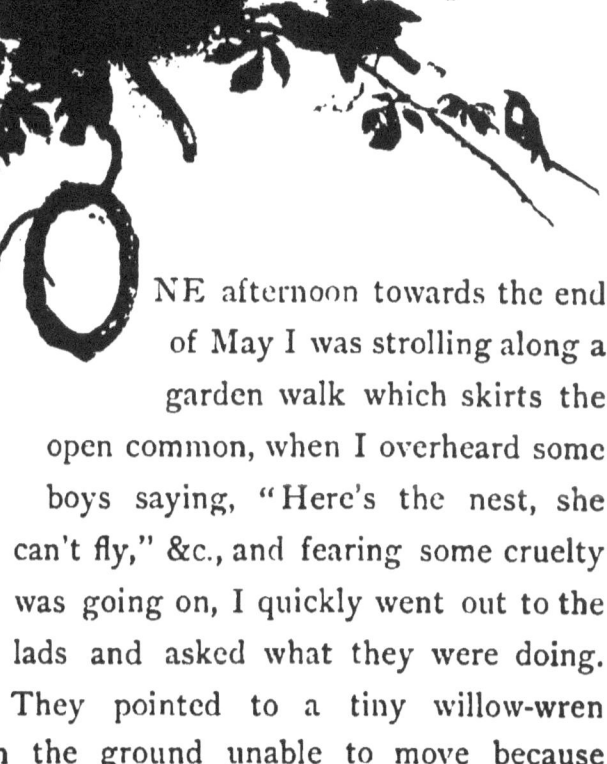

NE afternoon towards the end of May I was strolling along a garden walk which skirts the open common, when I overheard some boys saying, "Here's the nest, she can't fly," &c., and fearing some cruelty was going on, I quickly went out to the lads and asked what they were doing. They pointed to a tiny willow-wren sitting on the ground unable to move because her wings were glued together with birdlime.

It was the work of some bird-catcher; he had

placed the sticky birdlime on bracken stems around the poor bird's nest, which was in a tuft of grass and heather, and as she alighted with food for her young ones she was caught and held fast.   It was a piteous sight!   The five hungry little nestlings were cheeping for food, the bright eyes of the mother-bird looked up at me as if appealing for help.   The boys were as grieved as I was; but what were we to do?   I could not let the poor victims die of starvation, so I resolved to take the willow-wren and her family home and see if I could feed the little ones and release the glued wings so as to give the mother-bird power to fly once more.   With great pains I did succeed so far that the bird could plume her feathers, and, after a few days, she could again use her wings.   I fed the young birds, and in this duty the tender little mother aided me, and would even take food from my hand and put it into the gaping beaks that were always ready for small morsels of raw meat or meal-worms, on which diet the young wrens grew and flourished, until I was able one fine day to release the mother and children and rejoice in the thought that their innocent lives had been saved from a cruel death.

I can but hope that no reader of this book would ever dream of catching our songsters with birdlime, but there is a form of cruelty of which thousands of ladies *are* guilty, and against which I, for one, shall never cease to protest until the hateful fashion has entirely ceased. How often I wish I could lead those of my own sex to think of the terrible suffering they are causing to millions of birds· as sweet and innocent as my little willow-wren. Can any one conceive my having had her killed and stuffed, and then placed as a trimming on my bonnet! The thought of the willow-wren's mother-love ought to make such an idea abhorrent to any gentle-minded woman. But cannot my sisters be brought to reflect that every wing and bird's body they wear on their headgear means the cruel death of a creature of both use and beauty that was enjoying its innocent life, and doing us only good by carrying out its appointed duties in God's creation? I cannot express the pain it gives me to see aigrettes, wings, and whole birds still so lavishly used in trimming hats and bonnets. Loving birds as I do, I cannot help pleading for them from time to time, in the hope that public opinion may have some influence, and ladies may learn at last to be ashamed to be seen decked with an ornament which proclaims them both thoughtless and unfeeling.

The willow-wren, one of the most useful of our insect-eating birds, abounds in my old garden, and keeps the rose-trees free from aphides and other pests. It chooses very unsafe places for its nest, the smallest tuft of grass being deemed a sufficient shelter. One such nest, I remember, was located two years ago close to the field road where my hay carts were continually passing. The brave little mother seemed to have no fear, but as a heedless footstep might unwittingly have destroyed the nest, some branches were placed round the spot for her protection, and I hope she succeeded in rearing her family.

It is a charming sight to see a party of willow-wrens methodically clearing the insects from a rose-tree. Like a band of tiny acrobats they flit about sideways, upside down, in and out, until every twig has been examined and all the prey secured, then, with happy chirpings, away they flit to the next tree to resume their useful operations.

The sweet, warbling song of this migrant seems a truly summer sound, for the bird seldom arrives until the middle of April, and leaves us again about the end of September ; its note therefore suggests sunshine and flowers and the hum of insect-life.

TAME DOVES.

"Was not the Dove the first of all the birds
Loosed by the patriarch from the stranded ark,
Which roved not idly o'er the new-born world,
But backward turn'd, though winds were whistling past—
Though palm-groves and the flowery mead allured—
And bore the olive-branch to glad *his* sight
Whose hand had smooth'd so oft its ruffled plumes."
LADY F. HASTINGS.

"Like to a pair of loving turtle-doves,
That could not live asunder day or night."
SHAKESPEARE.

TAME DOVES.

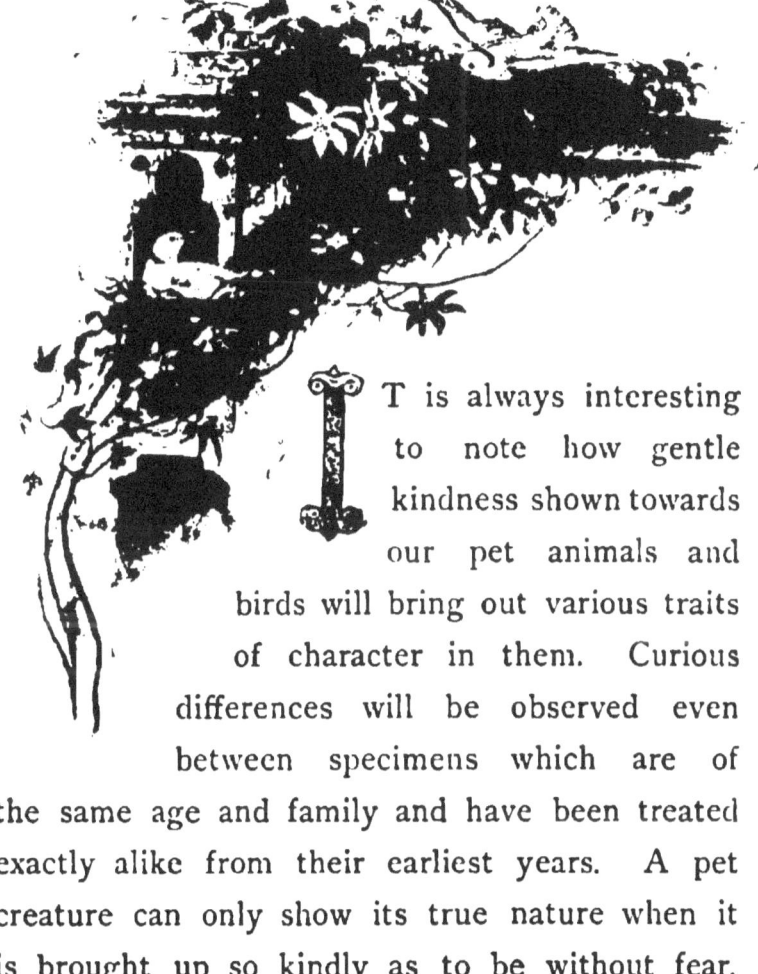

I T is always interesting to note how gentle kindness shown towards our pet animals and birds will bring out various traits of character in them. Curious differences will be observed even between specimens which are of the same age and family and have been treated exactly alike from their earliest years. A pet creature can only show its true nature when it is brought up so kindly as to be without fear. Alas, how seldom this is the case!

Almost all captive song-birds I have seen, excepting canaries, are sure to flutter more or less when any one approaches their cage, and this instinctive effort to escape shows timidity and unhappiness. I confess I could never find any pleasure in keeping a tiny captive which I knew was breaking its little heart in fruitless longings for fresh air and liberty.

To show what thoughtful kindness will do in creating happy confidence, I should like to relate the history of my tame doves, Peace and Patience.

These birds used to belong to a poor woman in our village; her only means of housing them was in a wooden box with a wire front. It was a wonder that they continued to live in such discomfort; yet, without a bath, a nest-box, or anything to make their lives pleasant or healthy, they showed the grace of patient endurance by living on with merely their bare allowance of food and water.

However, they were redeemed at last from their hard bondage, placed in a large wicker cage with plenty of suitable provender, enabled

to sun themselves in a pleasant verandah, and to
take a bath in pure water whenever they felt
inclined. Their plumage soon began to improve,
and became as smooth and soft as grey satin.
After a time they were let out to fly about in
the dining-room, and the male bird, Peace, might
often be seen sitting on the marble clock, gazing
at himself in the looking-glass over the mantel-
piece. I suppose he admired his own reflection,
for he would go again and again to bow and
curtsey and coo most lovingly to the bird he
saw in the glass, and never seemed to find out
it was all the while himself.

In spite of this foppishness he was a most
devoted mate, paying all kinds of tender atten-
tions to his gentle little wife, following her about
and often feeding her with any special dainty he
might come across.

Under these new and happy circumstances
Peace and Patience began to think of rearing a
family, and we found them searching everywhere
for materials wherewith to build their nest. Not
finding much that was suitable in my sitting-
rooms, they went to the flower-vases and began

pulling out the orchids and maiden-hair fern to line their nest.

It looked very pretty to see the little grey bird flying across the room with a great pink flower in her beak; but we thought a more suitable substance might be offered to them, and very gladly they welcomed some little twigs and dried grass, with which, after much cooing and confabulation, they constructed the family home. In a day or two a pair of snow-white eggs appeared, and then for a fortnight the little hen-bird sat patiently brooding over them, scarcely leaving them long enough to take her necessary food.

In due time we found two little doves were hatched. Small, pink, feeble-looking creatures they were; it seemed quite wonderful to think that they could ever grow up to be like their parents.

Patience was so tame that she would let me peep under her soft feathers to see how the tiny birds were progressing, and even if I took one of her children away to show to my friends she was in no way perturbed.

It is a great surprise to see doves feeding their

young ones. They take the tender little beak within their own and then pass the soft food, with which nature provides them at that time, from their own crop into the beak of the fledglings. The young birds seemed to have excellent appetites and grew rapidly, developing tiny quill-feathers all over their bodies, and in a few weeks they were clothed with soft grey plumage, so that we could hardly tell parents from children.

I have often heard doves spoken of as being less intelligent than other birds. On the contrary, my birds seem to think and almost to reason, as I believe my readers will agree when I tell them some of the clever things they have done.

One day when I was sitting in a room some distance from the verandah where the doves were, Peace found me out and came tapping with his bill against the window. I am always accustomed to attend at once to any such appeal from a bird or animal, since I generally find it to mean that they urgently require something.

In this case, as the evening was chilly, I let the three doves into their cage and brought it indoors; but I soon found all was not right, for the male

G

bird was greatly excited, apparently longing to
get out again, so I opened the cage door and the
window of the room, and away he flew. Presently
I heard Peace cooing loudly, and, following the
sound I found him under the verandah with the
young dove that was missing; he was evidently
trying to show me his truant child, and as soon as
I took them both up and carried them to the
cage, Peace was quite happy and content.

When the weather became warm and sunny
the little pair decided that their next nest should
be built in some clematis growing up the pillars
of the verandah. It was a charming spot to
select, for the little mother-bird had flickering
sunbeams shining upon her whilst she sat, and
leaves to shelter her from the heat.

Now again a domestic difficulty arose and
Peace came to tell me about it. What was he
to do for building materials? I provided small
flexible birch twigs, and was amused to find that
when I offered one, the little builder took it gladly,
and, flying off to the nest, presented it to his wife
and she wove it into the family dwelling.

Later on in the day it seemed to me that the

comfort of the home would be improved by some softer material than interlacing twigs, so I added a carpet of fine soft shavings; these also were quite approved, and after a time the nest was considered perfect. I felt inclined to call it our nest, as I provided the materials and was allowed to help in the building.

Two snowy eggs soon appeared, and then the parents took it by turns to sit upon the nest for about four hours at a time. This should teach us a beautiful lesson of unselfishness, for it must seem a little hard to have to sit still hour after hour and see another bird able to fly about enjoying the air and sunshine. I think my dove was well named Patience, but doubtless the strong feeling of mother-love made it easy, and the affectionate little father-bird seemed always ready to take his turn in the domestic duties.

The first heavy shower after the nest was built made me rather anxious for the comfort of the sitting bird; she would soon have been soaked with rain, so I racked my wits to devise a shelter. With some contrivance I managed to fix a slanting roof of stiff cardboard so as to keep

off rain and scorching sunshine. By talking
quietly to my pet she seemed quite to understand that she was not to be alarmed, and sat
calmly on her nest whilst I fixed her shelter.

The bird that is off duty is fond of coming to
visit me in the house. I am quite accustomed to
see a dove sitting amongst my working materials ;
I have even found an egg lying on my writing-
table as a modest gift and token of affection
from my gentle Patience.

Peace looks very pretty when he perches on
a white marble bust in the drawing-room. He
dearly likes investigating anything fresh, and I
once found him in the museum busily pulling an
old nest to pieces, because it contained some
materials he thought would be desirable for his
own home.

I learn many lessons from my little doves. I
see how affection begets confidence. These little
creatures trust me perfectly, and that gives me
true pleasure, and makes them very dear to me.
I think it is thus our Heavenly Father would
have us show our love to Him. He says, "I
love them that love Me," and the text goes on

to say, "and those that seek Me early shall find Me."

Then let all the dear young people who read about my doves try to learn, from their history, how they can please God by showing their love and trust in Him, by going to Him continually with all their difficulties, not doubting that He will hear, and abundantly answer their prayers.

FEEDING WILD BIRDS IN WINTER.

"Blithe Robin is heard no more :
  He gave us his song
  When summer was o'er
  And winter was long :
He sang for his bread and now he is fled
  Away to his secret nest.
  And there in the green
  Early and late
  Alone to his mate
  He pipeth unseen
  And swelleth his breast.
  For, as it is o'er,
Blithe Robin is heard no more."

ROBERT BRIDGES.

FEEDING WILD BIRDS IN WINTER.

NY winter's day a charming
sight may be witnessed outside the long French win-
dow of my drawing-room, but
this is especially the case in
frosty weather, when the frozen-
out birds come in flocks to par-
take of my bounty. Virtue is
its own reward in this instance,
for I derive untold pleasure
from the lively scene which greets my eyes when I

sit down each morning to carry on the dual occupation of writing letters and watching the birds.

This winter (February, 1895) is one of exceptional severity. More than a month of intense

MY WINDOW VISITORS.

frost will have killed thousands of birds, especially of the insect-eating species. Tits have even attacked the woody galls upon the oak-trees, and extracted the grubs from them, thus doing the forest-trees good service.

It is curious how plainly individual character

comes out in hungry birds. Nine robins are now, whilst I write, carrying on a guerilla warfare, pecking and flying at one another like little furies, as indeed they are. Much as I love robins, I must own they have villainous tempers, and will treat their own kith and kin with persistent cruelty.

Now a dozen or more fussy starlings have arrived for their breakfast, and eagerly pick up the coarse oatmeal, which seems to suit the requirements of most birds when they cannot get their own special diet. I like to listen to the busy chatter the starlings keep up all the time they are eating; it is varied by little tiffs, which constantly arise, when two birds spring into the air, peck at each other furiously for a moment, and then, the insult being avenged, drop down and resume their breakfast until there comes a scare about something, when away they all rush. Starlings are good emblems of perpetual motion — cheerful, busy creatures, they never seem to have a minute to spare, and make so much ado about both work and play that they are amongst the most amusing of the visitants to my window. Blackbirds, on the contrary, are sedately stolid, and usually keep in one position until their hunger is appeased, or, if compelled to fly off in the middle of their repast, they have the forethought to carry away a lump of bread or fat, which they can enjoy in private.

As a rule the thrushes stay away from my food supplies until they have exhausted other stores, but when they do join the throng of pensioners and accept outdoor relief, it is with a calm, fearless air, as if they had a full right to the choicest morsels. When all the rest take flight at some sudden noise, the thrushes generally remain and go on feeding with quiet dignity, as if quite above the silly frights of the vulgar herd. The busy scene would lose much of its interest without the calm effrontery of the blue tits. They perch upon the lumps of fat, assuming every possible attitude of graceful agility, and those who trench upon their domain have occasion to learn that their absurd little beaks can be exerted with considerable force and effect. The snowy lawn which forms the background to my bird-picture is a real "study in black and white." About fifty rooks are either feeding under the tulip-tree or walking about on the frozen surface of the snow. Hardly

FIR-TREE IN WINTER.

any bird shows the inner working of its mind so clearly as the rook. One may learn from its actions the dawning of an idea and the subsequent working out of the same.

One of these birds is at this moment weighing pros and cons as to whether it would be safe to join the party at the window. Whilst all are feeding quietly it decides to come, and marches slowly on; then, when the starlings take one of their sudden flights, the rook stops, looks this way and that, and feels doubtful. However, a second rook joins the waverer, and the two take courage and advance together. One of them stands on a lump of suet and breaks off pieces with its huge beak — the rook sharing with other birds the universal love of fat — the lump becomes smaller and smaller, and at last the great beak grips it firmly and away flies the rook, closely pursued by a crew of sable comrades, who are all eager to share in the spoil which they were not brave enough to secure for themselves.

I have not spoken of the sparrows; their name is legion. And how they do eat! No other bird clears away the food so quickly. The sparrows do

YEW-TREE SEAT AND WEEPING BIRCH.

not move more than they can help, and peck with the utmost rapidity, as though absolutely starving.

I suppose one ought to pity a "frozen out" sparrow as much as any other bird, but I could wish there were fewer of them at these times when one wishes to befriend the rarer kinds of the birds, and, if it were possible, reserve the food mainly for them instead of the plebeian sparrows.

The kind of provision I find best and most suitable for all tastes is coarsely ground oatmeal, Indian corn, hemp-seed, sultana raisins, chopped-up fat of any kind, and boiled liver cut up finely.

The raisins attract the wild pheasants, and it is a truly beautiful sight to watch these birds feeding quietly near the window, with the morning sun glancing upon their lovely sleek plumage until they look as if made of bronze and gold. During the autumn I have sacks of acorns and beech-mast collected and laid by until the birds are distressed for food, and then a large basketful is scattered daily beneath the tulip-tree upon the lawn, to the great delight of rooks, jackdaws, pheasants, and wood-pigeons. Even two moorhens from my lake have come up through the fields and remained for the last two months, not only feeding with other birds on the lawn, but visiting the poultry yard, picking up grain with the fowls, and several times they have also roosted in the henhouse. The lovely grey and orange nuthatches haunt the dining-room windows, where they share the nuts which are daily bestowed upon the squirrels.

This place, with its surrounding woods and gardens, where all birds have been protected and encouraged for the last twenty years, naturally abounds with feathered fowl of many kinds, but in most gardens, even somewhat near a town or city, birds may be coaxed to come by constantly placing attractive food where they can pick it up without danger from cats. This is best arranged either in a basket hung at a window or in a box fastened to a high pole. Any one may find pleasure in watching the various kinds of birds flying to and fro, and, for an invalid, it would be adding a charm to daily life, besides doing a kindness to a useful tribe of creatures which are too often persecuted rather than jealously protected, as they ought to be, in return for the valuable services they render to the gardener and agriculturist.

H

STARVING TORTOISES.

" Where'er he dwells, he dwells alone,
Except himself has chattels none,
Well satisfied to be his own
     Whole treasure ;
Thus, hermit-like, his life he leads,
Nor partner of his banquet needs,
And if he finds one, only feeds
     The faster."

VINCENT BOURNE.

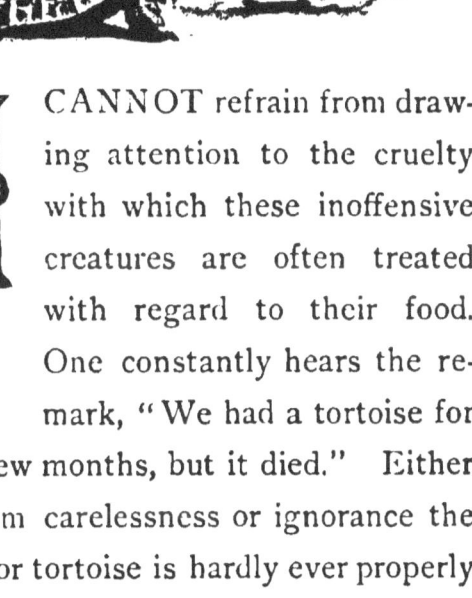

I CANNOT refrain from drawing attention to the cruelty with which these inoffensive creatures are often treated with regard to their food. One constantly hears the remark, "We had a tortoise for a few months, but it died." Either from carelessness or ignorance the poor tortoise is hardly ever properly fed, and, though it can endure privation for a longer time than most creatures, yet unless food is supplied it must die miserably of starvation at

117

last. The ordinary land-tortoise feeds on cabbage,
sow-thistle, lettuce-leaves, and dandelion flowers,
while some specimens will enjoy bread and milk as
well. I have been carefully watching a tame one
in my conservatory, and find that, day after day,
he eats a lettuce nearly half his own size. If,
then, he requires so much food to keep him in
health and vigour, how pitiable must be the condition of those kept without food, or those that
are perhaps offered a dandelion flower once a
week !

The water-tortoises are equally ill-used, for
often from lack of knowledge they are constantly
offered vegetable diet which they cannot eat, their
proper food being the live creatures they find in
the water they exist in. They are best fed in
captivity by supplying them with little portions
of raw meat, or remains of boiled cod or turbot.
They are easily distinguished from the land-
tortoises by their livelier movements, and by their
being able to swim in water. Still even they do
not care to be always afloat, so there should be a
piece of cork or some small island upon which
they can rest when they are tired of swimming.

One day I saw on a shelf in a village shop a handsomely marked tortoise-shell, which I rather desired to purchase for my museum. Upon inquiry I found it had been bought for a few shillings from a man who was going through the village with a truck-load of these poor creatures for sale. The shopkeeper knew nothing about the requirements of his new acquisition, and thought it would be quite happy in the water-butt, where he placed it for the night. It being a land-tortoise, it was of course found dead in the morning — one of the many victims of well intentioned ignorance. Those who sell tortoises in the streets know nothing about their habits, they only want to get rid of their stock as quickly as possible. The purchasers may never even have seen a tortoise before, and have not, as a rule, the vaguest idea of how it should be treated, so that the unfortunate creatures are almost sure sooner or later to perish miserably of mismanagement and starvation.

They are entirely vegetable feeders, so that the idea that a tortoise will clear the kitchen of black-beetles is an absurd fiction, though it is, I believe, urged by street sellers of tortoises as an inducement for the householder to purchase his stock.

One day a tortoise was brought to me by a man who said he had picked it up in one of my fields. I felt sure it must have strayed from its rightful owner, and we therefore made every inquiry amongst our neighbours round about in order to discover, if possible, its previous home. As no one would own the tortoise, we placed it in the conservatory that we might be able to observe its ways and habits, as it happened to be the first specimen of the kind that had been enrolled amongst my pets. When placed on the lawn for exercise the creature would greedily snap off every hawkweed flower he came to, and as these abounded in the turf he had happy times feasting on flowers and basking in the sun.

After keeping the tortoise about a year, it happened that a policeman living in a neighbouring village called here to see a friend of his, and this comrade (one of my gardeners) took him to see the flowers in the conservatory. After a few minutes the policeman exclaimed, "Why, there's our Jack!" An explanation ensued, and it turned

out that the tortoise had really belonged to him,
as he proved by showing a little hole he had bored
through the shell in order to tether Master Jack
and prevent his straying away. The tortoise had
been the gift of a dear friend, and the loss of this
pet had been quite a sorrow in the family. " My
missus will cry for joy at seeing Jack again," said
the man ; and very glad was I to restore the
truant to his rightful owner, whose pet he had
been for four years.

Although somewhat slow and inert, a tortoise is
quite worth keeping, and when well cared for,
properly fed, and taken notice of, it has a good
deal of a quaint sort of intelligence. The one I
now possess will feed from my hand, gives an
angry hiss when offended, will put on double quick
speed, when the door is opened, in order to elope
into the garden, and what mind he has is greatly
exercised about the lemurs. I judge this because
I so often find him gazing at them through the
wirework, his shell tilted at an angle as if he would
fain climb up to satisfy his curiosity.

To the poor people who often visit my place
in summer, many of whom have never seen such

a creature before, the tortoise is an object of surprise, not unmixed with fear, for one woman
asked if he would "fly at her," and others seem to
suppose him a creature of ferocious tendencies,
judging by the way they keep at a distance and
eye him askance.

I happened to be at the Zoological Gardens one
autumn day when some of the large Galapagos
tortoises were fairly active, and was fortunate
enough to see one digging a hole in a rather hard
gravel path. The excavation was carried on
entirely by the hind legs; first one and then the
other went down and grasped a few stones with
the claws on the foot; these stones were dropped
on the surface of the ground, and down went the
other leg, and slowly it brought up a little soil,
and this process went steadily on for ten minutes
or more, and the hole became about eight or nine
inches deep. The sturdy tail of the tortoise is
used as a sort of boring instrument in first beginning the hole, and when deep enough the
tortoise cautiously deposits her eggs at the bottom
of the cavity, and when all are laid the hole is
filled up with earth, well pressed down, and the

mother leaves her precious deposits to be hatched by the heat of the sun.

Gilbert White has remarked upon the tortoise as a weather prophet. He says, "As sure as it walks elate, and as it were on tiptoe, feeding with great earnestness in the morning, so sure will it rain before night." I can confirm this statement from my own observation, and when my tortoise walks in a weak sort of fashion, as if his limbs had no strength, it is a sure presage of fine weather. I frequently see another habit in my pet which is noticed in White's "Selborne": "He inclines his shell, by tilting it against the wall, to collect and admit every feeble ray." The sun shines upon the floor of my conservatory in different places according to the time of day, and my tortoise "improves the shining hour" by seeking these pleasant sunny spots and basking in them in rotation as the day goes on.

A young dove that is allowed to fly about in my conservatory is remarkably fond of the tortoise, and may often be seen sitting on its back and pluming itself; it stays there whilst the tortoise walks about, apparently quite unaware that it is carrying an "outside passenger."

In the Japanese islands these creatures grow to an enormous size. I possess a shell which is highly polished and ornamented with gold lacquer work; the measurement of it is three feet one inch by three feet four inches across, and, as these animals live to an immense age, this specimen may probably be several hundred years old.

As each year appears to be marked by a ring round each plate of the tortoise-shell, much as one sees them in a section of tree stem, it might have been possible to reckon the age of my huge shell, but in polishing the surface the rings have been effaced, so its age can only be conjectured.

Let it not be forgotten that a tortoise is a thirsty creature, and needs to have access to water in some very shallow pan out of which it can drink. My own specimen knows well the sound of falling water, and goes beneath the hanging baskets in the conservatory after the gardeners have soaked them, and there enjoys the dripping moisture, drinking from the pools upon the oiled floor.

The shell of a tortoise should be well oiled every few weeks, as it is apt to grow too dry, and might be liable to crack or peel off, the artificial life the creature leads in confinement tending to have a desiccating effect upon the shell.

If each reader of this book would kindly tell those who possess tortoises the kind of food they require it would greatly tend to reduce unintentional cruelty.

TEACHING VILLAGE CHILDREN TO BE HUMANE.

"Hast thou named all the birds without a gun?
Loved the wood-rose, and left it on its stalk?
At rich man's tables eaten bread and pulse?
Unarmed, faced danger with a heart of trust?
Oh, be my friend, and teach me to be thine."

EMERSON.

"Else they are all — the meanest things that are,
As free to live, and to enjoy that life,
As God was free to form them at the first
Who in His sovereign wisdom made them all.
Ye therefore who love mercy, teach your sons
To love it too."

COWPER.

"A man who is kind to the animals belonging to him will be thoughtful of the feelings and wishes of his family. A woman who, with patience and tenderness, cares for the domestic creatures around her home, can but be loving to her little ones; for she must observe how strong is the mother-love in the humblest thing that lives."

MRS. F. A. F. WOOD-WHITE.

TEACHING VILLAGE CHILDREN
TO BE HUMANE.

O much preventable cruelty in this world arises from ignorance that it seems the duty of every one to try and pass on to others any useful knowledge they may happen to have acquired, and thus increase the general sum of happiness in the hearts and lives of those who live around them. This general axiom is, I think, especially true with reference to information about animals and birds : we can prevent a great deal of cruelty being unintentionally shown towards the useful creatures that serve us in so many ways by using our influence wisely in the village schools and in the houses of the children's parents.

If some one in each country village would but gather the children together as often as possible, and talk to them pleasantly and kindly about the right treatment of horses, asses, dogs, cats, birds, &c., the little lads who will grow up to be grooms, ostlers, and carters, would be likely to remember the teaching they receive, and carry it out in humane treatment of the animals under their charge. I dare not repeat what I know of the cruelties practised by young boys upon birds and their nestlings in the breeding season, but will at any rate try and show some of the motives that lead young people to persecute birds and destroy their eggs. I would classify these motives thus : first, wanton mischief ; secondly, ignorance ; and thirdly, collecting mania. The two first mostly influence the poor, and the last the richer classes. I will endeavour to suggest remedies for each.

Mischievous country lads may in some measure be restrained by bills freely posted about in their village stating clearly the penalties for taking nests and eggs, with a list of protected birds. The notices should be couched in simple words, that children can understand, and not after the style of a notice board, which was placed to protect a spring of pure water for village use, and which ran thus: "Persons are requested to refrain from polluting or contaminating this water." I am afraid the rustic Tommy would not be much enlightened by these formidable words. Much more to the point is the warning to be met with in one Surrey village, "Children, let Well alone."

Any proved case of pure mischief or cruelty shown towards any living creature should be made a serious offence, rebuked openly in the village school, and spoken about to the parents by the clergy and others. In this way public opinion may by degrees be created, and any child so offending may learn that he or she is in disfavour for such acts.

It may be that only a few children out of a whole school have the disposition which delights in cruelty, but all are more or less ignorant and thoughtless, and need to be carefully and patiently taught the duty of kindness to all living creatures.

What constantly happens is this. A boy sees something unusual flitting about in a tree; he wonders what it is, and, wishing to find out, he naturally flings a stone at the object; when the coveted thing lies gasping at his feet he looks at it a moment, and flings it aside. He knows nothing about the harm he has done — has no idea that he has killed a bird that perhaps very rarely visits our shores, and that may not be seen again for years. Why, then, if we wish such rare visitants to increase, do we not systematically teach our boys and girls to watch and study the ways of wild creatures, and feel some rational interest in them, so that in consequence they may be drawn to do what they can to aid in their preservation? The children need to be instructed about the life-history of one bird after another; information should be given about its mode of life, its usefulness in destroying insects, its nesting habits, the tender love between the mated birds, and their care of their young — defending them even at the risk of their own lives if needful. Surely the impressible hearts of children might be led to pity and protect our feathered songsters if once they were made thoroughly acquainted with facts such as these.

Leaflets on natural history and kindness to animals and birds can be had very cheaply from the R.S.P.C.A., the Society for the Protection of Birds, and the Dickybird Society, and these should be scattered broadcast throughout our land, where they cannot fail to do beneficent work. If coloured lithographs of our common birds were hung up in village schools, and simple explanatory lessons were given upon them, it would surely be more useful to our country children than that they should be taught to know the exact difference between the Indian and African elephant! And yet one often sees large prints of foreign animals in schools, and but seldom anything so simple as pictures of the animals and birds the children meet with in everyday life.

Again, small prizes might be offered for the best papers written upon our English birds, describing their habits and uses, and all the facts about them which the children are able to comprehend.

I was delighted to receive from a dear unknown child a capital drawing of a brambling which I could recognise at once, so truthful was the pose and colouring, and, though the young artist was only eleven, his .drawing and letter revealed a born naturalist. Now this kind of effort might be largely promoted amongst young people with excellent effect. We should make a rule I have myself observed all my life most carefully, "Never to have a bird killed wantonly, even for drawing or study purposes." There are admirable pictures to be obtained of all our English birds, and, with an occasional find of a dead bird, and the glimpses we may obtain of them in life, these will furnish enough to guide young artists in their first attempts. Suppose the children of a village school awakened to this kind of competition, and a "tea" given to those who have sent in papers, I can see the way to a delightful evening when the papers should be read, comments kindly offered, mistakes corrected, information given, and some fresh subjects set for the next time. The whole village would be full of chat about this gathering, and each child would naturally bring much of the knowledge gained into his own home, and thus the parents would indirectly become enlightened upon natural history subjects, on which they are usually deplorably ignorant.

These humble suggestions are offered as being the best means I can at present bring forward in order to attain the end we have in view, and in a measure they apply equally to young people in a higher position in life, who would, I believe, welcome little informal meetings for the reading of the papers they may have written, and the attainment from their elders of further information on the life-histories of animals and birds. I earnestly hope that still better plans may be evoked from others as a result of bringing this subject prominently forward.

I must draw attention to an excellent idea borrowed from Miss Carrington's book on "The Extermination of Birds," and it is that our young people who desire to possess collections of birds' eggs should be encouraged to model them in wax and colour them precisely according to nature.

Even the one egg used as a model need only be borrowed from a nest and returned when the model is cast and coloured; or one may be lent for the purpose from the collection of a friend. The young artist would be able to enjoy the thought that his specimens were of a permanent nature, and that there had been no rifling of the nests of valuable birds, without whose incessant labours we should have endless insect plagues. For the *modus operandi* of this last idea I would refer my readers to Miss Carrington's little book.[1]

In trying to discourage the collecting mania I know I am treading upon delicate ground, and I must define my meaning clearly, else I may convey wrong ideas and provoke needless discussion of vexed questions. I do not think very young children should be allowed to kill any living creature in order to make a collection — it must tend to make them hard-hearted; far better is it to lead them to watch and admire every bird and insect they come across. As they are taught to know the ways and habits of living things, and

[1] "Extermination of Birds," by Edith Carrington. Wm. Reeves.

year by year they grow up with kindly feelings towards them, I think they will hardly be amongst those who would destroy perhaps fifty lovely butterflies in order to complete a circle of colour in some case of insects. *That* is the kind of collecting I wholly condemn as both useless and cruel. So much study can be carried on without taking life, that it seems undesirable to adopt in early life any line of investigation which involves the death of the objects being studied — at any rate until the student is old enough to avoid any possible cruelty in the matter. It appears to me that if we bring up young people with a reverent love for all, even the lowliest of God's handiwork, that feeling will tend to restrain them from exercising the instinct of destruction which we may often trace in children's early years.

There must be a certain amount of slaying for necessary food, and animals and birds prey upon each other by the very laws of their existence. Specimens, too, are required for museums, else how could students learn to know the various orders of animal and bird creation ; but outside all these unavoidable uses, the indiscriminate slaughter of innocent life that is carried on year by year, fills me with distress, and I, for one, shall never cease to protest against it with voice and pen. I can but hope that by the multiplication of our Selborne branches and kindred societies we may in time see some diminution of this selfish warfare against all creatures in fur and feathers.

STUDYING NATURE.

"If thou art worn and hard beset
  With sorrows, that thou wouldst forget,
  If thou wouldst read a lesson, that will keep
  Thy heart from fainting and thy soul from sleep,
  Go to the woods and hills !—no tears
  Dim the sweet look that Nature wears."

LONGFELLOW.

STUDYING NATURE.

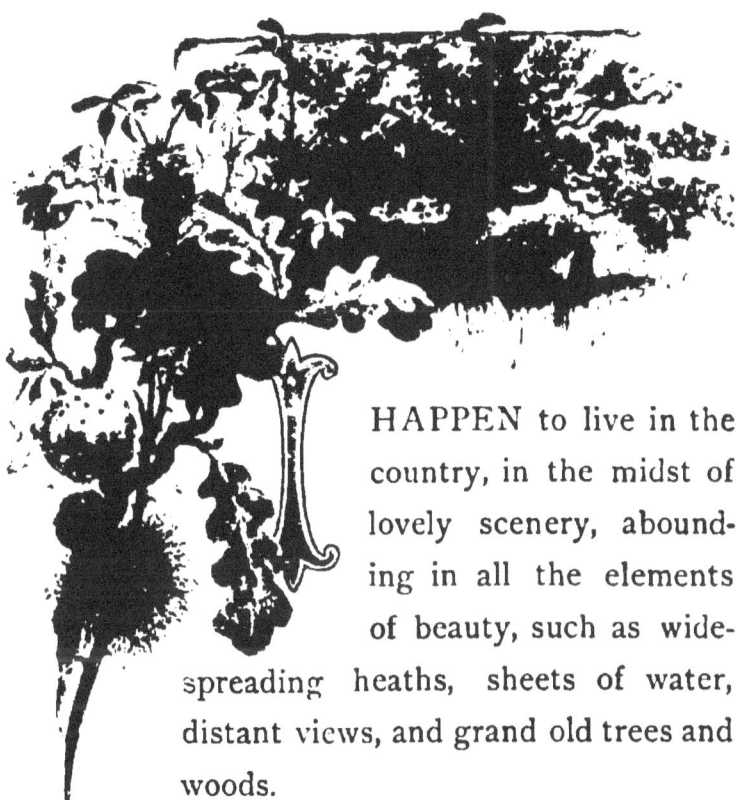

HAPPEN to live in the country, in the midst of lovely scenery, abounding in all the elements of beauty, such as wide-spreading heaths, sheets of water, distant views, and grand old trees and woods.

There are many varieties of birds and insects to be seen, plenty of wild flowers, mosses, and lichens in the lanes, and in my own grounds all kinds of cultivated flowers.

Numbers of young people come to stay with me

in the course of the year, and naturally, when I am taking walks with them, and we are admiring trees and flowers, or a sweet-voiced bird begins to sing, questions arise about the names of various plants and songsters. I confess I am often surprised to discover the very limited knowledge of elementary natural history or botany that is possessed by young girls who in other branches of study are intelligent and well-informed. It grieves me to think that the instructive book of Nature is thus disregarded, and its lessons left unlearned, by thousands who would be much happier, and have many more resources to fill up leisure moments, if they knew more about the everyday things which surround them in the country.

Even if it is the lot of many young people to live in towns, still, when they pay visits to their friends at the seaside, or in the country, there are ample opportunities for natural history studies, and by means of books these studies can be carried on when they return home.

I will try and describe one of the subjects which my young visitors always discover to be full of interest, namely, the study of trees.

Such a book as "The Forest Trees of Britain"[1] will supply the names of all our ordinary trees; and, when taking a ramble in a country lane or garden, if a perfect leaf of each species of tree is gathered, well pressed, and dried between sheets of blotting paper under a heavy weight, there will be found pleasant occupation for some wet day spent indoors in arranging these specimen leaves in a large blank book.

Space should be left to write the English and Latin name of each tree, whence it was imported, and some of its chief uses. If, later on, the autumn-tinted leaf of each species can be obtained, and a coloured drawing made of its catkin flower, then in time a really charming and valuable book will be formed, which a girl will feel pleasure in showing to her young friends, and thus others will be led to fill up their leisure time with instructive pursuits of this kind.

Drying and arranging the leaves is only the first step towards a more intimate knowledge of this subject. The exquisite beauty of autumn-tinted leaves attracts the attention of the most unobser-

[1] By the Rev. C. A. Johns. S.P.C.K.

vant.   One longs to preserve them, and for years
I used to try various methods of pressing and
drying them with but very partial success.   Now,
however, I have devised a plan by which their
fleeting colours are so exactly imitated that my
friends constantly mistake the painted leaf for the
real one.   As it may afford pleasurable occupation
for some of my readers, I will briefly describe the
process.

The materials required are but few: a common
slate, some fine drawing paper, a cyclostyle [1] roller,
and a bottle of the ink which is sold with it.   A
small quantity of the ink should be placed on the
slate, and the roller passed to and fro until it is
slightly and evenly inked.   The leaf should then
be placed on a flat, hard surface, and the roller
passed firmly over it so as to leave a little ink on
the under side of the leaf to mark the veins.   The
leaf should then be reversed, with the ink side
downwards, on a piece of drawing paper, and the
roller firmly passed over it once or twice.   The result will be an exquisite faint imprint of the exact

[1] This kind of roller and the ink can be obtained at any
stores.

shape of the leaf with all its veins. After a few
minutes it will be ready to be tinted in water colours,
so as to exactly resemble the various hues in the
real leaf. The colours should be very moist, and
rather floated into each other, as in this way one can
most readily attain the delicate gradations of tone.
When finished the leaf should be neatly cut out
with fine scissors, carefully following the outline of
the notches, which vary so much in different trees,
and give character to each species. When such
painted leaves are gummed into a blank book the
effect will be found to be wonderfully real. The al-
bum should be large enough to allow of four or five
leaves, each representing a different stage in the
coloration — yellow, pink, crimson, and all other
tints which belong to each special tree. A page
should of course be reserved for each set of specimens, and the English and Latin name, the date, and
any other particulars written at the bottom of the
page will add to the scientific value of the collection.

The various galls which are found on each
species of tree will alone furnish a wide field
for study. The ink with which I am now writing
is the product of an oak-gall which is imported

K

in large quantities from Asia Minor; many kinds
are of great value in dyeing; and the life-history
of the numerous gall-flies is most curious and
interesting.

Careful drawings of the buds of trees as they
open in spring will reveal the delicate plaiting of
the tiny leafage within.   We can then discern how
some leaves are folded lengthways or in half, others
curled up spirally or fluted; we shall see how the
embryo leaves are protected by more than a dozen
scales, often lined with silky down, and then, as in
the case of the horse-chestnut, still further guarded
from the winter's cold by an outer coating of resin.

Again, the fruits and seeds of trees would prove
an interesting subject.   I wonder how many young
people know the difference between the English
sycamore, which is a true maple, and the sycomore
of Palestine, which is a fig-tree; and yet they are
totally unlike each other — the first producing a
dry seed vessel, and the other an eatable fruit;
the sycamore usually having a stem twenty or
thirty feet high before it branches, and the sycomore dividing near the ground, so that Zaccheus
found no difficulty in climbing its ample stems.

There are some birds which frequent special trees, and are named after them, such as the hawfinch, the whinchat, which is found on its favourite furze-bushes (called whins in Scotland), the pine and fir grosbeak, and the nuthatch. The student should know something of these birds and their habits, as being linked with the trees they frequent.

There are innumerable insects also found upon the leaves and stems of trees. It has been calculated that about two thousand different species of caterpillars and larvæ of various kinds prey upon the oak alone.

We thus see vistas which open out before the young student, any one of which, when followed up with thoughtful perseverance, will add immensely to the pleasure of walks abroad and quiet hours at home.

As this chapter aims to be a suggestive one, I would mention the possibility of making a dried collection of the trees of Scripture. This may seem at first sight very difficult of attainment, but we often hear of friends going abroad (even if we cannot go ourselves), and a request to gather and

dry a spray of olive or carob-tree will hardly be
refused, and thus in time, by the help of others,
our collection will be formed, and will become of
much value to us in teaching our Bible classes, as
well as from the associations the book will have
with the kind travellers who remembered us when
far away.

I greatly treasure my own specimens of oleander
gathered on the shores of the Lake of Galilee, the
carob-leaves from Bethlehem, sycomore fig from
Jericho, pomegranate from Jerusalem, and olive-
sprays from the Garden of Gethsemane.   Pleasant
hours have been spent in reading about each tree,
and the passages in Scripture where they are mentioned are invested with a deeper interest from
one's knowledge of many facts connected with
each which otherwise would have passed un-
noticed.

For instance, the fruit of the carob or locust-tree
may have been the food of John the Baptist ; it is
known to this day by the name of "St. John's
Bread," and the sweet, nutritious pods are still
eaten by the poorer inhabitants of Palestine.   It
is also more than probable that "the husks that

the swine did eat," mentioned in the parable of the
Prodigal Son, were the long curved pods produced
by this tree [1]; and it is also well known that the
equal-sized, hard-shelled seeds of the carob were
the original "carat" weights of the jeweller.

Thus we see how many interesting facts cluster
around the name of a single Scripture tree. If a
spray or leaf of any of the kinds mentioned is
placed in the centre of a page, with some neatly
written texts referring to interesting facts about
its history and uses, we shall then have always at
hand a delightful book, which will prove useful for
many purposes. It will afford plenty of subjects
for conversation when we wish to make Sunday
afternoon a bright and happy time for some young
people, kept indoors, it may be, by wet weather.
Many a sick person's weary hours might be
cheered by such a book being lent, and in endless
ways it will well repay the trouble of putting it
together.

A collection of seedling trees, carefully dried
between sheets of blotting paper in a press or

[1] To this day great quantities of these husks are imported
into England for the purpose of feeding cattle.

under a weight, then fastened into a blank book with strips of gummed paper, with the English and Latin names to each, and a note of the age of the seedling, will form a pleasant memento of our forest rambles, and probably may lead on to further study of the same kind.

Lemon and orange pips will grow readily in damp moss under a glass, and can be transplanted into pots of earth, so that seedling plants are attainable even by those who live in towns. I was much surprised to find that tamarind seeds taken out of the jam would grow very quickly in cocoa-nut fibre if kept moist and placed near a hall stove. The secret appears to be that although the tamarinds are packed in barrels, and hot sugar is poured over them, yet owing to the thickness of the seed-coat the life principle is not destroyed.

To make our collection complete there should be seedlings of the other great division of plants, namely, those with only one seed-leaf, such as palms, cannas, bulbs, grasses, &c. A few date-stones kept in moist earth, and placed where they will have a slight degree of regular heat, will supply one of these specimens, and Canna seed,

Indian corn, and other plants of the kind, grown in the same way, will supply other examples.

Whatever branch of nature-study we select, or whatever collections we may decide to make, the invariable result is that our interest in that special thing becomes immensely deepened ; we begin to notice points that never struck us before, our power of observing becomes quickened, we really begin to think we must have been almost blind hitherto not to have been aware of the new and curious things we are daily finding out, we learn that the natural world around us is a storehouse ready to yield endless treasure to those who are willing to seek it, and thus I have often noticed that when once young people can be induced to begin a collection of some sort it is the first step to their becoming true nature-students.

Mothers often long for some simple occupation for the little busy fingers, that get into mischief if unemployed, and what can be more innocent than collecting and pressing wild flowers and leaves, and, when dried, arranging them in a book, so that mother can write the name to each specimen and talk about them, telling the uses to which some plants are applied? In this way children grow up to be ardent botanists, and may learn a great deal about the science without any of its dry details being presented to them in the shape of long unpronounceable terms, until they are old enough to see for themselves the necessity for them.

I have tried to indicate a few of the ways in which young people may study Nature, but the avenues into her domain are endless; let us at least endeavour to traverse such of them as may be within our reach whilst we are young, and so make our lives all the brighter and happier for knowing something of the wonders of this marvellous world in which it has pleased God to place us.

INSECT OBSERVATION.

"In this enchanted leisure
The only restless thing
Is one loose ray of azure,
A dragon-fly on wing;
The rustling of its flight
Is like the sound of light."
EDMUND GOSSE.

"Throngs of insects in the shade
Try their thin wings, and dance in the warm beam
That waked them into life."
W. C. BRYANT.

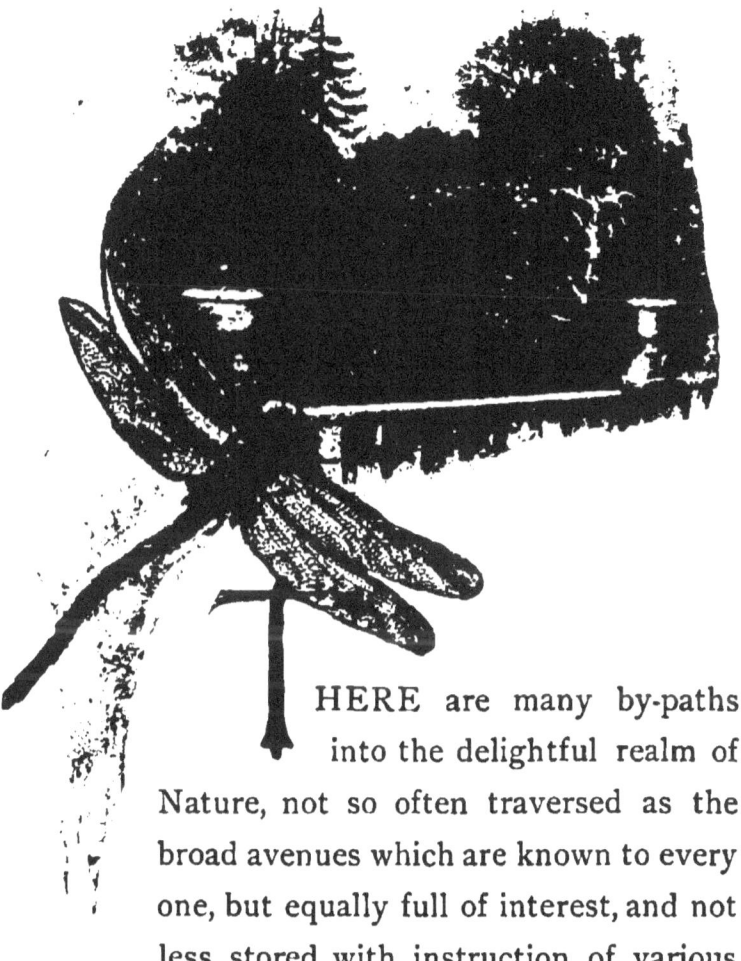

HERE are many by-paths into the delightful realm of Nature, not so often traversed as the broad avenues which are known to every one, but equally full of interest, and not less stored with instruction of various kinds. One of these paths I follow almost daily, and with ever-increasing delight. It happens that there exists, close to the garden-room where I usually sit and write, a valley, with winding grassy paths and banks of azaleas and rhododendrons. It is a quiet and secluded spot, and has been so for the last twenty years.

Generations of birds have nested in its shrubberies year after year; bees know well that the spot is rich in honey-laden flowers; insects that they will be undisturbed there save by the blue-tits and other fly-hunting birds. Mosses and lichens carpet the moist, shady banks on one side, whilst bright sunshine glistens on the opposite side through the greater part of the day. There could not be a more favourable spot for insect observation, and this is the special by-path to which I would direct the reader's attention to-day. One frequently hears the remark, "I should like to know more about the habits of insects," and the question often follows, "How can I best study them?" To this I would reply by describing what is to be seen and learned in my valley.

This will not pretend to be a scientific description of insect life, but simply a quiet glimpse at the habits of several kinds of winged creatures disporting themselves with such native ease as one can never see when they are caught and caged and brought indoors. Having placed a chair in the shade, facing a sunlighted bank of evergreens, laurels or rhododendrons, we must keep absolutely still, closely on the watch with a small field-glass in our hands for at least half an hour if we desire to see and study the insects that will visit the flowers and leaves. As we walk casually round a garden not very much can be seen except the bees upon the blossoms or an occasional dragon-fly. Almost every species of fly darts away at the approach of man ; their eyes are so marvellously observant of any moving object that we can learn hardly anything of the life-history of the various species unless we remain perfectly quiescent long enough for confidence to be restored, or, in other words, until the insects forget our presence and are again at their ease.

Hot sunshine seems to afford perfect bliss to almost every kind of fly, and in that condition · we see them basking on leaves in great profusion. Bluebottles, the golden greenbottle, the drone-fly, all the highly coloured, swift-darting sunflies — these are constantly to be found poised on the laurels, although only for a few moments' rest between their aerial games. It gives one a sense of pleasure to watch anything so absolutely happy as these creatures seem. Three or four will start off at once for a frolic, whizzing through the air, performing a sort of "ladies' chain" evolution, each seizing the other for a rapid whirl or two, then, exchanging partners, faster than the eye can follow them they skim through the air, and finally return to their leaves to rest. Each species has its own style of flight. The sunflies have the power of remaining motionless, poised in air for a considerable time, whilst they watch any object that interests them. Their wings vibrate so rapidly as to be invisible, but if you attempt to catch one with a net, away, with a dart, the fly is off into space only to return in a moment as if to mock your clumsy attempt to capture it.

Now your attention is arrested by the quivering antennæ of a long-bodied fly that is stealthily prying into leafy crevices, seeking for some living object, a caterpillar or chrysalis, into which it may insert its egg. The grub when hatched will feed upon the living substance of the caterpillar, which survives for a time, until eventually the grub attacks some vital part. This kills the caterpillar, but not before the grub has changed into a chrysalis, out of which will emerge in due time an ichneumon fly, ready to victimise other insects in the same way.

On the broad leaves of a low-growing plant some female wolf-spiders have placed themselves, each carrying her bag of eggs beneath her body. There they will bask for hours; possibly the warmth of the sun tends to mature the eggs, the treasure for which they seem to live. These spiders will allow themselves to be killed rather than part with that little cream-coloured ball. Truly the spider offers a marvellous instance of maternal love ! After a time the eggs are hatched, and then the mother may be seen with her whole progeny clustered upon her back enjoying their sun-bath. The first time I saw this family event I could not understand why the back of the spider had suddenly become grey and furry, until I brought a magnifying glass, and then I could plainly discern the minute offspring covering the mother's body.

Now a glittering dragon-fly darts down the grassy alley seeking its prey. It, too, rejoices in the sunshine and poises lightly on the tip of a leaf between its flights to enjoy the welcome beams. These huge flies adopt a particular haunt, and will remain there hawking up and down day after day. I often become acquainted with individual dragon-flies from seeing them so often : I know where to find them on sunny days. If they are unmolested and you move gently enough they will allow you to approach them closely, and I believe in time they would take a fly from your fingers. There is hardly a more beautiful insect than *Æshna grandis*, one of the largest of our native dragon-flies. In life its eyes glisten like opals with changing colours, its long body is a marvel of bluish green and black mosaic markings, and its four lace-like wings are fit to adorn the Queen of the Fairies.[1] It is hard to convince people that

---

[1] "And forth on floating gauze, no jewelled queen
　　So rich, the green-eyed dragon-flies would break,
　　And hover on the flowers — aerial things,
　　With little rainbows flickering on their wings."

JEAN INGELOW.

this is a perfectly harmless creature; yet it does not bite, it has no sting or venom of any kind, and the long body which writhes about as we hold it can hurt neither men nor horses, although it is vulgarly known as a horse-stinger. Possibly we may be favoured with a glimpse of a dragon-fly's toilet if we keep still and motionless. The brilliant eyes are softly brushed with one of the forelegs, so as to clear away any speck of dust ; the wonderful head, which seems attached to the body by the merest thread, turns this way and that as the insect plies the combs or short, stiff fringes with which its legs are furnished, brushing its finery as carefully as any human dandy could, till body, head, and wings are all in perfect order. Then it will sail away with a scarcely perceptible move-ment of its broad wings to pursue its living prey, a veritable pirate of the air.

The various seasons bring, of course, a suc-cession of insect visitors to my valley. In early spring the solitary bees are a great delight to me ; they are the species which exist in pairs, not often in communities, as the honey-bee does. Great masses of lungwort (*pulmonaria*)

L

being out in flower in April and May, all kinds of insects are then to be found upon it, seeking honey or pollen among the blossoms. By closely watching and comparing the specimens I see with plates in the books on bees I have learned to distinguish many of the different species. It is one thing, however, to see a bee figured in a book, or to look through a dried collection of them ; it is far more delightful to see the bright, beautiful creature itself, instinct with life, busily at work or play. These solitary bees evidently enjoy flirting in the gayest manner, and their soft, downy bodies and brilliant colours only show to real advantage whilst alive and lighted up by sunshine. It is a great puzzle to make out the different species, especially when, as in some cases, the sexes differ much in appearance. A jet black bee was often to be seen in early spring hovering over the pulmonaria, more intent on his companions than on the flowers, and every now and then he would seize a yellow-bodied fellow-worker, and off the two would go for a frolic in the air. I became enlightened when I found they were husband and wife, and merely beguiling the tedium of work by an occasional excursion together to the other side of the valley.

Some years ago I was greatly puzzled by an insect which seemed to appear and disappear in a strange manner; it flashed across a shady path like a minute firefly — an intermittent fleck of snow — it never seemed to settle anywhere, and was altogether incomprehensible. At last I succeeded in catching some specimens and solved the mystery. The little creature proved to be a slender fly with a tapering, pointed body clothed with fine silky scales, which in some positions were white as snow with the changing iridescence of mother-of-pearl; thus in its ever-varying flight the insect appeared and disappeared according as the rays of light fell upon it at different angles. In size the creature is but small, less than a house-fly, but when magnified its beauty is exquisite — the wings decked with rainbow colours, the thorax rich emerald green, and in life the eyes also greenish and opalescent.

I might go on endlessly describing visitants to my favourite haunt and yet always have something interesting to say about them, but I hope enough has been noted to prove that insect observation has its keen delights.   To a wearied brain it is a quiet mode of refreshment which will commend itself to all who give it a trial on a summer day in some sheltered garden ; but the observers must possess the requisite qualities, namely, patience, gentleness, and a true love of natural history.

SOLITARY BEES AND WASPS.

"Hide me from day's garish eye,
While the bee with honey'd thigh,
That at her flowery work doth sing,
And the waters murmuring
With such concert as they keep
Entice the dewy-feather'd sleep."

MILTON.

"The wild bee's note that on the wing
Booms like embodied voice along the gale."

HOGG.

SOLITARY BEES AND WASPS.

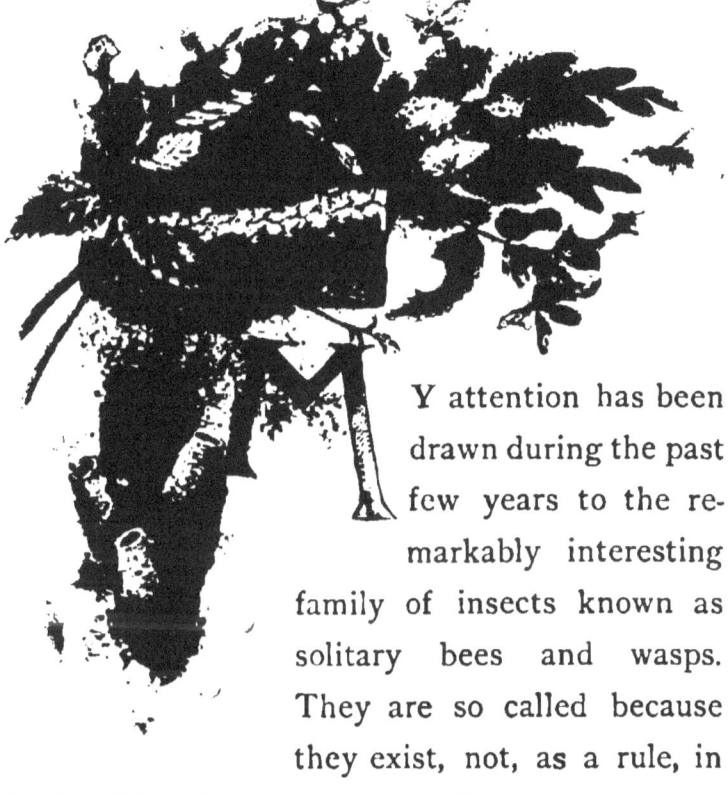

Y attention has been drawn during the past few years to the remarkably interesting family of insects known as solitary bees and wasps. They are so called because they exist, not, as a rule, in colonies like the honey-bee and common wasps, but singly or in pairs.

These insects may often be seen in our gardens feasting on the flowers, boring tunnels into our gravel walls, making curious little nests in holes or angles in the brickwork of our houses, and yet comparatively few people know much about them and their habits, partly because they may often be taken for honey-bees, and without very close observation it is difficult to learn the characteristics of the different species.

I will endeavour to give a few details about some of the solitary bees and wasps which have come under my own observation; but it is a large subject, and as my variable health will not allow me to travel or even drive far from home, I can only speak of those specimens I have met with in my own grounds, and of which I have made a small collection for reference.

COLLETES.

(ONE THAT PLASTERS.)

This species forms a tunnel in the ground from eight to ten inches deep, and this space is divided off into about seven cells. The wonderful thing is the way in which the cells are lined with a

strong membrane like gold-beater's skin, yet ex-
quisitely fine, and lustrous as a piece of beautiful
satin. The bee has a forked tongue which she
uses like a trowel, smoothing down each layer
of the silk which she deposits on the walls of
the cells, plastering three or four layers one over
the other till her children's nursery is upholstered
quite to her mind. She then goes off to the
flowers and labours diligently until she has made
up a little ball of pollen and honey; one of these
balls she puts in each cell and lays an egg in it,
out of which a tiny grub will be hatched in due
time. Finding its food all ready, the grub eats
and grows until it is full-sized, then it turns into
a chrysalis, and at length comes out a perfect bee
like its mother.

The Colletes are smaller than the honey-bee,
but at first sight are very like it in colour and
shape. The males are smaller than the females;
they do nothing towards founding the family; they
flit from flower to flower and fertilise the blossoms,
so that in this way they are of great use by
enabling plants to produce seed; they also bask
on leaves in the sun, and seem to have a happy

though very idle time. This seems to be the case with the males of all species of bees. The females are the hard workers; they make the home, lay the eggs, collect the pollen and mix it with honey for the food of the young when hatched, and then they hibernate through the winter so as to be ready to begin their work again the following spring.

There are five species of this bee, and they choose different places for their nests according to their species. Some like a sunny aspect, some choose shady places, some bore into the face of sandy rocks, others into the mortar in old walls, but wherever it may be, there are generally multitudes of them to be found in the same place, each one having its separate hole, but dwelling in large colonies.

This bee has three great enemies : two of them are a bright-coloured bee, called Epeolus, and a fly, Miltogramma, either of which will go down the hole in the absence of the bee and lay its egg in place of the rightful owner. These usurpers turn to grubs and eat up the food which has been prepared for the Colletes. The third enemy is the earwig; if *it* once gets in, it will eat up the egg, the food supply, and the bee itself. In this way the bee is kept in check, else we may suppose it would multiply far too abundantly.

ANTHOPHORA.

(FLOWER-RIFLER.)

This is a name that would apply to most bees, but certainly this one seems unusually energetic in obtaining honey, visiting each flower in succession, and then whisking off to the next flower-bed as if it had not a minute to lose.

The male is jet black, and hums loudly all the time it is on the wing. It has a very long tongue, beautifully fringed with hairs at the end to enable it to sweep the flower-tubes and drink in the honey. It is a most difficult bee to catch, its vision being so acute that it is off like a flash the moment it sees the net; it is therefore only after many attempts that one can secure a specimen. The female is very different in appearance, being densely covered with yellowish down, and is easily known by her second pair of legs which are very long and clothed with tufts of black hairs. Its nesting habits are the same as those of Colletes, only the grubs remain in the cells all through the winter and hatch out in the spring.

There are immense numbers of these bees on Hampstead Heath, and it is said to be the species alluded to by Gilbert White, of Selborne, as existing in colonies on Mount Carburn, near Lewes, and so bold is it that when people walk near its nests it will rise on the wing and dash against the faces of the intruders. One species of Anthophora makes its cell on dry walls, where it looks like a lump of mud, as if a handful of wet roadstuff had been thrown on the brickwork. These bees are clever little masons and use sand, earth, chalk, and woody material, mixed in different ways, to form the nurseries for the eggs they purpose to lay.

I have not as yet been able to find one of these nests, but I read that they are about an inch deep, of the form and size of a lady's thimble, finely polished, of the colour of plaster-of-Paris and stained in various places with yellow. These insects have to work very hard scooping out clay from one bank, obtaining chalk from another, and sand from the path or elsewhere, and then these materials have to be moistened with their own saliva and made up into pellets of a size that they are able to carry on the wing, and so by slow degrees the walls of the cell are built of these tiny bricks all glued together by their own cement. Inside there are cells with eggs and bee-food placed ready for the young grub when it is hatched.

MEGACHILE.

(LARGE-LIPPED.)

One day in summer I saw a bee go into a little hole in the brickwork of our house, and knowing it was probably making a nest, I waited till it came out and then caught it with my net that I might find out its species and then let it

go. I found it was the very interesting solitary
bee which lines its nest with rose-leaves (*Mega-
chile Centuncularis*).   It is a rather handsome
large insect, covered with brownish-yellow down,
and has furry-looking legs.

It is called sometimes the upholsterer-bee, because it uses such delicate curtains for its nest.
I used to think it was the pink rose-petals that
it used, but I have since found out more about
its ways, and often see where it has been at
work on my rose-trees by the circular holes it
makes in the green leaves. It settles on the
edge of a rose-leaf, and holding it firmly between
its fore-legs it saws out a round piece of it, then
flies with it to its nest and puts it neatly in as
a lining. It takes from nine to twelve pieces to
form a cell, and they are pieced together without
any cement or glue so that, as they dry, they
form a neat little tunnel. In this the bee stores
up the honey and pollen of thistles which form,
when mixed together, a sort of rose-coloured con-
serve or jam, and then in this it lays its egg and
closes up the end of the cell with three pieces of
leaf exactly joined so as to fill up the entrance.

In this way it works till the hole is full of cells, then finally closes it up and leaves the nursery to manage for itself. The leaves of the birch-tree, elm, and dog's mercury are used by other species, but they all choose some kind of leaf to line their nests.

ANTHIDIUM.

(A DWELLER IN FLOWERS.)

This is another pretty bee which chooses a hole in some tree-stem which has been made already by a beetle or boring insect, and in order to make things quite comfortable for her future family she goes to the woolly hedge-nettle or the wild lychnis, and scraping off the wool she rolls it into a ball and flies to her nest with it, then she unrolls the wool and lines the sides of the hole with it, thus making a warm soft nest in which to place her eggs and the store of pollen and honey which they will require.

ANTHOCOPA.

(A FLOWER-CHOPPER.)

I have not succeeded in capturing this very rare bee, but it is said to have been found both in Scotland and England. It has a great liking for colour, for it makes choice of the petals of the wild scarlet poppy with which to line its nest. It bores into the hardest paths by the side of corn-fields and then cuts little pieces out of the corn-poppy flowers and curtains its nest with them, and, like all the rest, it provides a store of food, lays its eggs, and then closes up the hole.

OSMIA.

(SWEET SCENT OR PERFUME.)

This genus is so called because some species are said to throw out a sweet odour when they are touched.

There are about ten species of these bees in

M   VARIEGATED DEODAR.

England, and we must look very carefully if we wish to find their nests.

One kind of Osmia will scoop out the pith from a piece of bramble-stem and make cells in it composed of minced-up bits of wood or leaves. Another kind will choose an empty snail-shell and fill it up most cleverly with little cells to hold her eggs. A third species of Osmia thinks a keyhole is a most suitable place for her nursery, and will so fill it up with plastered earth, eggs and pollen, that the lock is rendered perfectly useless.

HALICTUS.

(TO CROWD TOGETHER.)

This curious bee prefers to work after the sun has gone down, especially on moonlight nights. Like the Colletes, it is fond of building in colonies.

They burrow into the ground about eight inches, working in such crowds that it is difficult to avoid treading upon them. They seem able to manage with very little rest, for after all this night-work they are equally diligent in the daytime collecting pollen in which they lay their eggs at the bottom of the tunnels. These bees have very beautiful wings, rich with all the colours of the rainbow, but, as they are not very large, a magnify-ing glass is needed to enable one to see these colours to advantage.

One of this species is the smallest bee in England; it would almost be taken for a house-fly, but for its long antennæ. The most beautiful specimens may often be found upon the flowers of the chickweed.

ANDRÆNA.

There are seventy species of this bee, and their habits are much the same as the other bees I have mentioned, but this genus is the victim of a most strange enemy — a small winged beetle called Stylops.

The grub or larva of the Stylops is found in dandelion flowers, and when the bees come seeking honey these little creatures climb on to the bee,

and, worse than that, they creep into its body, and
there they live and grow, feeding on the inside
organs of the bee until they are fully grown, when
they turn into chrysalides.

Kirby, the great naturalist, was, I believe, the dis-
coverer of this wicked little insect.   He saw a small
lump on the under side of an Andræna bee, and on
taking it off with a pin he found to his surprise
a queer insect with milk-white wings and two
staring black eyes peering out of this lump—and
this was the perfect Stylops, hatched from the
body of the poor bee, which, strange to say, was
not killed by the parasite, but appeared to suffer
pain and irritation when the Stylops came out
between the joints of its body.   It seems as if
almost every bee and wasp has a special enemy
created to persecute it.   We may sometimes see
upon our window-sills in summer a very brilliant
little creature called the Ruby-tailed fly.   When
the sun shines upon it, it looks like an emerald sus-
pended from a bright polished ruby with a pair of
wings, so brilliant is its metallic colouring.   There
are five species of this insect, and they all prey
upon mason bees and wasps, creeping into their

cells and laying their own eggs with those of the wasp or bee, which are of course destroyed by the grub of this cruel intruder.

A French naturalist writes that he saw a Ruby-tail fly go into a Solitary bee's nest in a hole in a wall, and when the bee came back she found the Ruby-tail, and had a desperate fight with her. The fly is able to roll up into a ball as a hedgehog does, but this did not save her, for the bee sawed off her wings, and, dragging her out of the nest, threw her on the ground, and went off to get some more pollen. Poor Ruby-tail was not going to be beaten; she climbed slowly up the wall into the bee's hole, and there she succeeded in laying her eggs before the rightful owner returned, so after all the bee's family were not saved by the mother's brave defence of her nest.

The Cuckoo fly is another species that victimises bees and wasps in the same way, and the large tribe of ichneumon-flies are always on the watch to lay their eggs in any living things that will suit their purpose. They possess a long, flexible tube called an ovipositor, and by means of this they can insert their eggs inside wasps' and bees' eggs, and

even into chrysalides and live caterpillars the cruel
fly will drive this tube, and leave her eggs where
they will hatch, and live until they are full grown,
feeding on the living substance.   I have sometimes
kept caterpillars hoping they would turn into
beautiful butterflies, and instead of that I have
only had a crop of ichneumon-flies because their
eggs, unknown to me, had been previously laid in
the bodies of the unfortunate caterpillars.   You
may always know an ichneumon-fly by its quivering antennæ; they are never still for a moment
while daylight lasts, and the fly itself may also
be known by its long, slender body with a hair-
like waist.   Some of the species are so minute
that they lay several of their eggs within a but-
terfly's egg, and it affords quite enough food for
the ichneumon-grubs until they are full grown.

Others again are large insects with such a long
and powerful tube that they can pierce through
solid wood in order to reach the concealed grub in
which they desire to lay their eggs.   I believe the
largest of the species measures four inches from
head to tail, the ovipositor being an inch and three-
quarters long.   While I am speaking of parasites

I may mention the clever way in which a humble-
bee will sometimes rid itself of a species of mite
which one may see swarming on its body. I give
this on the authority of Rev. Mr. Gordon, of
Harting. He says that the bee seeks an anthill
on which it throws itself on its back, and sets up
a loud buzzing noise; the ants soon take the
alarm, swarm out of their nest, and at once fall
upon the bee; but the latter simulates death,
stretching out its limbs rigid and motionless; the
ants therefore leave it alone, and seizing the mites
which are running over its body, they soon dis-
patch them all, when the bee gets up, gives itself
a shake, and flies away happily relieved of all its
tormentors.

WASPS.

I will now touch upon the habits of a few of the
Solitary wasps.

It happens that my house is a favourite nesting-
place for them. Some years ago I noticed small
cells made of grey mud placed in some of the
angles of the brickwork close to our drawing-room

window, and seeing that some were like little pockets half open, and others closed up, I was led to watch and see what was going on.

A slender kind of wasp, a species of Odynerus, marked with black and yellow stripes, came with materials in her mouth, and began working on some of these mud cells against the wall; she kept on, hard at work all day at her masonry.

At last I thought I would open one of the finished cells and see what was inside, so with a fine penknife I broke away part of the cell wall, and there I found a number of greyish green cater- pillars' half killed and unable to move. Down at the bottom of the cell was the wasp's egg, and the instinct of the mother insect leads her to obtain these caterpillars, and in order that they may be in fit condition for the grub when it hatches out of the egg, she gives each of the caterpillars a bite which paralyses it but does not affect any vital part, so it lives on in a helpless condition, and the wasp grub literally eats its way through the cater- pillars till it is full grown, then it turns to a chrys- alis, and after a time it becomes a black and yellow wasp like its mother.

It is curious how tame insects will become if treated kindly. I used to know these little wasps quite well, and if they came into the rooms, and I found them on the window-panes they were quite accustomed to be placed gently outside that they might go on with their nests. A nephew of mine who holds a position in some sugar works at Cossipore in India, tells me in one of his letters that the air in the factory is so filled with wasps and hornets attracted there by the scent of the sugar, that they constantly strike against his face as he walked about. The workpeople and clerks take all kinds of precautions against them, wearing leather leggings over their trousers and beating them off continually; they get frightfully stung and tormented all day long, whilst my nephew, who is fond of all living things, takes no precautions at all, has never injured the insects, and never once had a sting from them. This shows that insects can discriminate between friends and enemies.

In my nephew's own house some wasps came in and formed a nest in his dining-room on a wall bracket within a foot or two of his usual seat at dinner, and they too were perfectly friendly and would settle on his face and hands, and never think of stinging their friend.

I remember once in a country village seeing a man hard at work thrashing corn in a barn, and quite near to him there was an immense hornets' nest hanging from a beam. We asked if he was not afraid of them, but he smiled and said, "Oh, they know me well enough ; one of 'em fell inside my shirt t'other day, but he was very ceevil and never stung me, for I never interferes wi' them, so they don't interfere wi' me."

Many years ago a curious thing happened in a friend's house in Surrey. In a spare bedroom which was not often used, there was a small Pembroke table with two flaps which could be put up or down. The maid had to get the room ready for a visitor, and in dusting the table she lifted up one of the flaps when down fell a quantity of dry earth all full of whitish grubs and chrysalides, and a few young wasps were also crawling about. It was found on examination that a solitary wasp had gained some mode of access to the room, and had made her family nest under the flap of the table, and unless it had been thus happily discovered the room would soon have been full of young wasps, much to the discomfort of the coming visitor.

One of the mason wasps called Odynerus not only makes a tunnel a few inches deep in the ground, generally in sandy banks, but it builds a kind of little tube of grains of sand glued together and places it just over the hole. It curves a little to one side, and is very possibly intended to act as a protection against various flies and parasites that would try to creep down and lay their eggs amongst those of the wasp.

This wasp stores up grey caterpillars for its young as the mason bees do, so we see that they have their use in tending to reduce the number of larvæ which prey upon our vegetables, and should be protected on that account.

An old silver-fir at the Grove, which had become decayed in the centre, became a home for countless thousands of a small species of wasp ; they scooped it into endless galleries and cells, and filled them with half-dead bluebottles and other flies to serve as food for their grubs.

I sat and watched them at work for half an hour one day, and saw that about every half-minute a wasp arrived, each one holding some kind of fly in its mandibles; as I imagine this went on from early morning till dusk we may easily reply to the frequent inquiry of, What use can wasps be in the world? and why were such troublesome insects created? by pointing to the useful labours of this despised creature in reducing, not only the destructive grey caterpillars which abound in our gardens, but also the swarms of flies which beset us in the summer months.

We had to take down this great fir-tree, as it was completely decayed and likely to fall with the next high wind, and when it was felled we saw the marvellous work the wasps had been carrying on — the stem was completely honeycombed with wasp-cells and all through that summer endless numbers of wasps continued to hatch out of the old tree-stem.

The mason wasps are a very serious evil in Florida and many other hot countries, because of their tendency to fill up every convenient crevice with their mud nests. For instance, a gun may be laid aside for a day or two without a cover, and a mason wasp will at once fill up the barrel with mud, and when the owner, all unsuspectingly, puts in the cartridge and attempts to fire the gun, it will probably explode, and possibly cause the death of the sportsman. Many a lock is rendered useless, and all kind of domestic troubles are caused by this persevering insect.

I may here say a word about the wasps I have had to deal with in Switzerland. I used often to find their pretty little nests, about the size of a small rose, made of a grey papery material, fixed on various objects, frequently on stones by the roadside, on tree-branches, or on the walls of houses and churches.

I brought one home and placed it in a sunny window of the hotel we were staying at. I had not noticed that the cells were full of young grubs, and one morning we came down to find the room full of lively young wasps which had hatched out of my nest, and we had to set to work and clear them away before we could eat our breakfast in peace. A friend has kindly lent me a somewhat similar nest she found on some heather in England.

I have now spoken of a few of our most common Solitary bees and wasps. There are hundreds of species, so that it is a wide subject and might be indefinitely extended.

If any young people desire to study these curious insects, I may mention a book which will be found very useful for identifying the species: "British Bees," by W. E. Shuckard, published by Lovell Reeve & Co.

With a magnifying glass one may see the two kinds of eyes with which bees are furnished. The two large eyes with hundreds of facets which we can easily see, are supposed to be for discerning objects near at hand. Then on the top of the bee's head are three little specks of eyes called "ocelli," placed in a triangle; these are believed to be for long vision, to enable the bee to guide its flight in the air.

A small lens is an essential thing to carry about with us, revealing a whole world of interest and beauty, which does not come within the range of our ordinary vision.

DRONE-FLIES.

"Nor undelightful is the ceaseless hum,
  To him who muses through the wood at noon ;
  Or drowsy shepherd as he lies reclin'd,
  With half-shut eyes, beneath the floating shade
  Of willows grey, close crowding o'er the brook."

JAMES THOMSON.

DRONE-FLIES.

(ERISTALIS TENAX.)

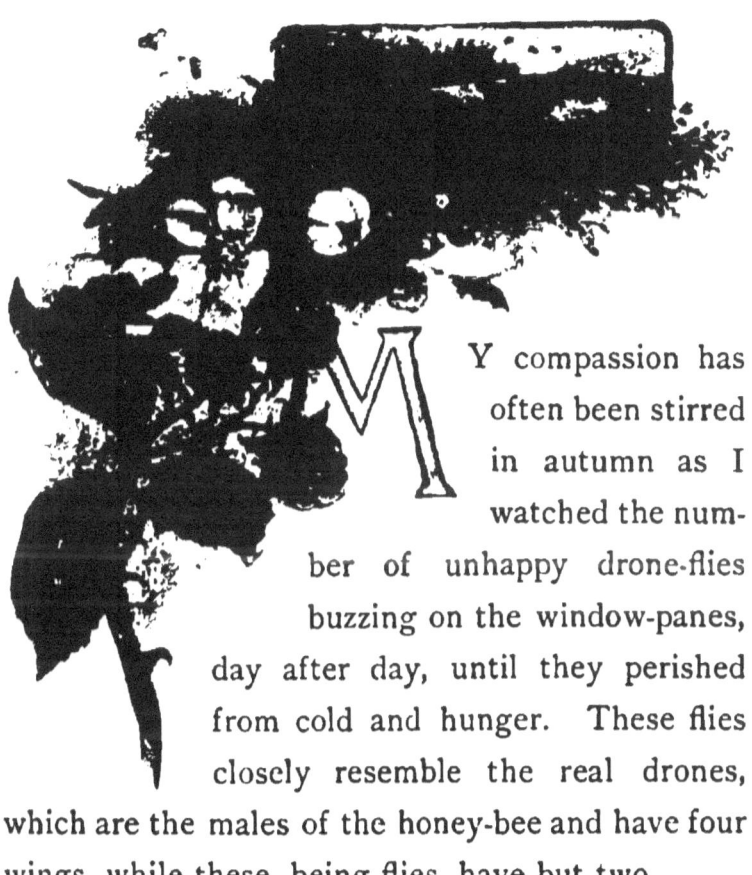

Y compassion has often been stirred in autumn as I watched the num-ber of unhappy drone-flies buzzing on the window-panes, day after day, until they perished from cold and hunger. These flies closely resemble the real drones, which are the males of the honey-bee and have four wings, while these, being flies, have but two.

They are large, handsome insects, with a downy, yellow-brown thorax and shining black body which moves up and down in a wasp-like manner. When flying about the room they keep up a loud humming noise, which at once betrays their presence.

As soon as cold weather begins these flies are driven to seek shelter in our rooms, where they find warmth, but usually no food or welcome. This year I thought I would prepare "a refuge for the destitute," in the shape of a small glass globe, with sufficient ventilation, a little trough full of honeycomb, and a small pan of water. Into this little home I introduced three of these dipterous "waifs and strays" I found buzzing on the window-panes last October, and I suppose they liked their quarters, for they settled down amicably enough, and spent their whole time, like many beings far higher up in the scale of creation, in eating, drinking, and sleeping! I can speak well of these drone-flies as pet insects, for they become absolutely tame, so as to come on my finger, and to bear being stroked with a soft feather. They cannot sting or bite, as they possess no aggressive weapons of any kind, and having proverbially nothing to do, they are very easy-going, happy little creatures, only asking for sunshine and food to keep themselves in health and contentment.

It is really a curious sight to watch the morning toilet of a drone-fly through a magnifying glass. After rubbing the various legs well together, the yellow down upon the head has to be attended to ; it is thoroughly combed by means of a row of small spines running down the fore-legs ; these are raised over the back of the insect, so that the spines are drawn through and through the soft, downy fur until it is in perfect order, the action reminding one irresistibly of the toilet of a human being.

The head is placed on such a slender pivot that it can be turned in every direction, and looks as if it would come off altogether as the fly turns it this way and that, and vigorously combs and brushes it in every part. Then the back and abdomen are cleansed from every speck of dust, and not until all this is accomplished does the insect seem to care for any food — thus setting to insects in general an excellent example of cleanliness.

Attracted by the tempting scent, the fly might often be seen upon the honeycomb, taking up the sweet contents of the cells with its long proboscis, which is not unlike an elephant's trunk, the honey being drawn up by means of flaps at the end which act as suckers.

Often have I watched my drone-flies and shown them to my friends, who never fail to be interested, and pronounce them remarkably curious creatures. Though so common, they are well worth observing in this way through a magnifying glass, for a casual glance will not enable us to see the full beauty of the eye with its endless facets, the structure of the legs and the spiny combs, or the beautiful yellow fur which clothes the thorax.

These flies of mine are let out in the room for exercise on fine days, and enjoy flying about in the sunshine. One of them remained out for a week or more, and when replaced with his friends he was seen to be thin and starved as compared to the others who had lived in plenty.

I often notice the great difference of character

that exists in insects. These drone-flies do not appear to be at all unhappy in captivity, they become so tame as to come on my finger and accept any suitable food placed there, and after they have been flying about they will walk into their globe as if perfectly content to abide in it. Not so the honey-bee. A specimen was on the window-pane one very wet and stormy day, and fearing it would die if I let it out of doors I introduced it among the drone-flies. They, good, easy-going creatures, were quite friendly towards the stranger, but the poor bee could not settle down — it fussed all day up and down the glass, despised the sweet provender, and, fretting, I supposed, at its absence from the community, was found dead next morning.

One day in January I gathered a spray of sweet-scented coltsfoot in flower, and placing it in a glass of water, enjoyed its delicious perfume. Supposing it might contain some honey and prove acceptable to the drone-flies, I let them investigate the flower, with the result that they speedily became covered with its white pollen. I feared this might clog their yellow down, and was about to brush it off with a feather, when I saw, rather to my surprise, that the flies were greedily devouring the pollen grains, brushing them off their downy bodies by means of the combs on their fore-legs, and then the flaps at the end of the proboscis rapidly picked up each grain until there was not one left. I am glad to know this fact about their diet, as I can now give the interesting pets both liquid and solid food, which will no doubt help to maintain them in health and vigour.

We will now turn to the larvæ stage of these flies when, as purifiers of the foulest putridity, they are doing us most essential service. The fly lays its eggs in the mud of some stagnant ditch, and out of each of them emerges a whitish worm-like grub with a long tail, which is its breathing apparatus, and must therefore always reach to the surface of the water. It is formed of grad-uated tubes, which can be retracted or drawn out exactly like a telescope. If the water is shallow, only one or two tubes are needed, and the tail appears somewhat thick, but if, owing perhaps to a sudden shower, the water deepens, then the creature can draw out tube after tube until the tail is two inches in length, and graduates to a thread-like point. If these grubs were thrown into deep water they would be drowned, being suffocated from want of air, but in ditches, where they are usually found, they can crawl along in the mud by means of very small legs on the thorax and abdomen, and ascend the sloping bank until they reach the needful air. Respiration is carried on by means of a double air-tube within the tail. When at its full expansion these tubes lie parallel to each other, but when the tail is retracted the tubes fall into two coils at the base, where it issues from the body of the grub — truly a marvellous piece of mechanism for such a lowly creature. The most noisome black mud is the favourite habitat of this rat-tailed maggot, as it is called, and to it we owe a deep debt of gratitude, since, repulsive as it may appear to our eyes, its life-work is to purify such foul places as would pollute the air we breathe ; it feeds and luxuriates upon that which is full of the germs of fever and mortality to us, and then, when full grown, it buries itself in the ground to come forth in due time as a bright-winged fly.

Even in its perfect state it is doing us service, for in seeking pollen for its food it helps to fertilise our fruit-tree blossoms, being seen upon them in the early days of March, long before other tribes of winged insects (excepting bees) are to be found abroad. The early spring sunshine attracts them from the nooks and corners where they have been hibernating through the winter, and greatly do they seem to enjoy rifling the newly-opened flowers of our apricot and peach-trees.

The specific name of Tenax given to this fly shows its power of clinging firmly to any object on which it settles. Each leg is furnished with a pair of strong curved claws which, when closed, appear to be like twelve grappling irons, and may well account for the tenacity of hold which the fly possesses. ·

From the interest I have found in keeping my drone-flies, I feel encouraged to try and learn more of the habits of other flies and insects. I believe in this way many curious facts may be ascertained about the life-history of many little-known species which are seen for only a limited period of the year, and whose further doings have not as yet been fully traced.

THE PRAYING MANTIS.

"O crooked soul, and serpentine in arts."

DRYDEN.

THE PRAYING MANTIS.

(MANTIS ORATORIA.)

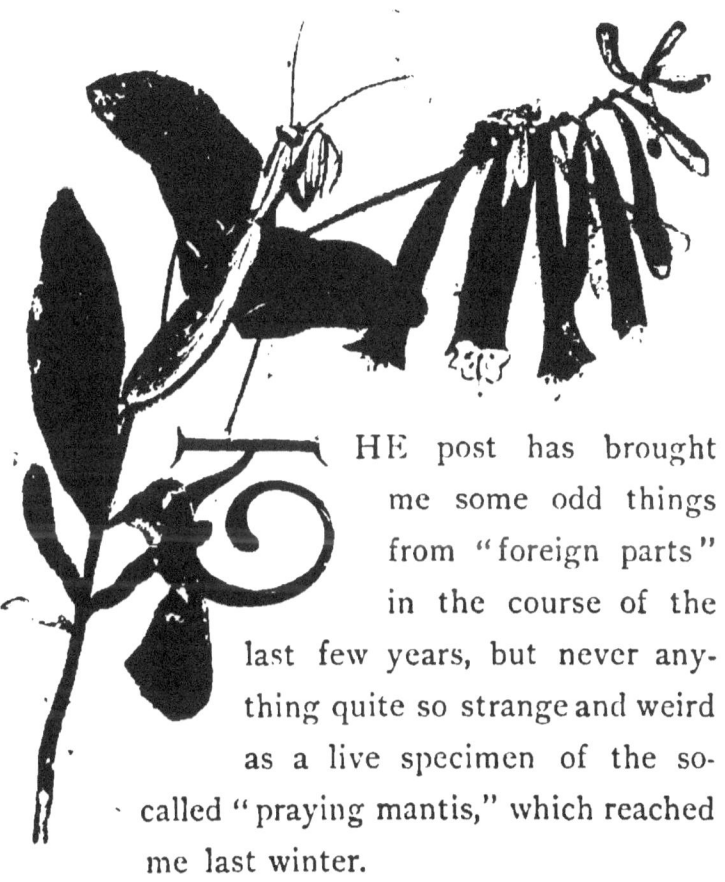

HE post has brought me some odd things from "foreign parts" in the course of the last few years, but never anything quite so strange and weird as a live specimen of the so-called "praying mantis," which reached me last winter.

This curious insect was sent from Mentone by

the same kind friend who forwarded the interesting sacred beetle, the "Cheops," described in
"Wild Nature."

The cold journey and lack of food had made
the poor mantis look so nearly dead that I almost
despaired of his recovery. The food of this tribe
of insects being flies of any kind, a bluebottle,
which happened fortunately to be on the window-
pane, was captured, killed, and presented to the
illustrious stranger, who feebly nibbled a portion
of his body, drank a little water, and appeared
somewhat revived. The mantis was then placed
near the fire, and we hoped that warmth might
prove restorative.

The mantis is never met with in England; it
is a native of the warmer parts of Europe, and
various species are found in the tropics. It is
a large and powerful insect, varying from three
to five inches in length; it has six legs. The four
legs which it uses in walking are long and slender,
while the pair nearest the head are much thicker,
and are armed with very sharp spines, with which
the mantis kills the insects upon which it feeds.

Its usual position is a sort of sitting posture,

holding up the fore-legs slightly bent as if in the attitude of prayer, and from this fancied resemblance the creature has gained the name of "praying mantis."

Deceit and cunning seem combined to a remarkable degree in the nature of this creature, as if to make up for the slowness of its movements. It will remain stealthily on the watch whilst flies are hovering within sight, apparently taking no notice, but secretly biding its time until a victim is within the range of its cruel enemy; then one swift stroke impales the fly upon the spikes of the fore-leg, which holds it fast in the pangs of death.

As Mr. Duncan wittily says in his charming book on "Transformation of Insects" : " Any unfortunate moths that may admire the mantis on account of its attitude of supplication soon find out that instead of saying 'Let us pray,' it says 'Let us prey!'"

When my specimen began to revive I could but gaze with wonder at the strange attitudes the creature assumed. Its head seemed to be set on a revolving pivot, for it could turn in all directions

with the greatest ease ; its limbs stretched themselves out at every conceivable angle, as if simu-
lating the twigs on a tree-branch.   Grotesque and
weird are the terms one would use in describing
this insect ; it seems a freak of nature, and quite
fascinates one by the oddity of its appearance.

I read that the Chinese keep these insects in
bamboo-cages, and take advantage of their quarrel-
some disposition by making them fight for their
captors' amusement.   Mantises are so pugnacious
that they will continue the conflict, hewing at each
other like hussars fighting with sabres, until one
or other of the combatants is killed.   Those who
have watched these engagements say that the
wings are generally expanded during the fight,
and when it is ended the conqueror devours his
antagonist.

Although we see that the mantis has no right
to its character for sanctity, I thought my specimen
ought to have an appropriate name, so he became
known in the family circle as Simeon Stylites!
The chief difficulty was how to keep him warm
enough through wintry days and nights ; this end
was, however, attained by keeping a night-light

always burning in his glass-case, and of course this led to some little teasing about my ever-lighted lamp at the shrine of my patron saint!

The second day after Simeon's arrival no flies could be had, so in despair I tried whether a meal-worm would be accepted instead. I was humbly presenting my newly-killed offering to what appeared a very meek and innocent creature, with its arms folded and its head on one side when, to my great astonishment, the deceitful thing suddenly sprang up and made such a vicious snap at my fingers that I dropped the meal-worm and retreated. That was my first lesson in the habits and manners of this holy hypocrite! for the future I learned to treat him with respectful caution, and handed his prey to him at the end of a pair of forceps.

It was a comical sight to see Simeon discussing a meal-worm. He found out that it was a tooth-some dainty, and accepted it very readily. Hold-ing it in one of his spiked fore-legs, and biting it piece by piece as if it were a banana, he munched away until he was satisfied, and then he generally tilted up the last portion as if he were draining a little beaker. I need hardly say that the meal-worm was mercifully killed first, else I could not have watched it being thus demolished.

The mantis seems to have remarkably keen sight and to be very watchful, for if I tried to touch anything in his globe he would face round instantly and stand on the defensive. If a twig was held near him he would throw out his long fore-legs and fight with the intruding thing, showing a dauntless spirit and very irascible temper.

I was most anxious to keep my curious pet alive; and, fearing I might not treat it rightly in all respects, I wrote to Mr. Bartlett at the Zoological Gardens, asking his advice about food and general treatment. He replied with his usual courtesy, but I was sorry to learn that, even under his experienced treatment, mantises never live through an English winter.

It is sad to record that Simeon grew less and less inclined to eat. In spite of all possible care he became inert and helpless, and died at the end of a week.

With the experience I have gained I should not quite despair of keeping a mantis alive throughout the summer and autumn. At that period of the year one could ensure suitable food and sufficient warmth to keep the insect living in health and comfort. It would be worth while to take pains to learn more about the life-history of a creature of such exceptionally singular form and habits.

o

THE CORK MOTH.

"'Faugh ! the claret's corked !' 'So it is, and very badly corked,' growls my lord."— THACKERAY.

THE CORK MOTH.

T may appear to many
readers a most unlikely
thing that even in our
sitting-rooms, on our window-panes, or in our wine-cellars
we should find subjects for study
in natural history, but I will try
to show that there is some truth
in such a statement.
We only need to be careful ·observers to be
rewarded from time to time by finding material
for thought and investigation in very unlikely

places. Not having ever lived in town, I cannot tell whether the creatures I purpose to speak about would be found there, and my remarks must, therefore, apply to country-houses and their visitants. If I had been told that a certain moth existed in my wine-cellar, and that by means of its larvæ burrowing into the corks some dozens of choice old Italian wines would soon ooze away and leave nothing but half-empty bottles, I should have been very incredulous. I had never seen such an insect in the wine-cellar in the past thirty years, and knew nothing of its existence.

I made its acquaintance, however, in the following manner. The plate containing the daily food of my mongoose is kept on a bracket just inside the cellar stairs. A cork had lain on this bracket for some months, and had apparently become glued there, for I could not detach or lift it. On close examination I found that this cork must have a tenant of some kind, for it was surrounded by fine particles, evidently gnawed by an insect. When a light was brought I soon found that a grub had been at work mining holes and furrows in the cork, and had then spun a very strong silky texture, by which it had firmly attached the cork to the bracket. Having made its home secure, it had gone on to spin a soft, silken cradle, in which I found the culprit itself ensconced.

This may seem but a trivial thing to record, but here was a life-history being worked out in small compass, all unknown to us in our daily business, and though in this particular case no harm resulted, yet by this apparently insignificant insect, as I afterwards found out, thousands of pounds are lost every year, its larvæ boring the corks, and thus causing the leakage of valuable wine, especially old sweet wines.

I was led to make inquiries about this cork moth, and a wine merchant kindly supplied me with the following facts : —

In twenty-five years' experience he had never seen the perfect insect, but knew it well to be a moth called Oinophila-v-flava. This creature finds its way into dry cellars and lays its eggs in the corks of bottles which are unprotected by wax or leaden capsules. A small white grub with a brown head is hatched from the egg, and bores a tunnel through the cork, just so far as to reach the saccharine in it, on which the creature feeds. When it has attained its full size it spins a silken case and turns into a chrysalis, from which the moth emerges in April and May.

Anxious to learn still more regarding this curious insect, I went to the Natural History Museum at Kensington, and by the courtesy of the authorities I was allowed to descend to the basement, where the long galleries are filled with insect collections. A case was brought to me which contained the Oinophila-v-flava, a long name, which I had expected would belong to a moth of ordinary size. What was my amazement, therefore, when I was shown a golden-coloured speck with four small wings, the upper pair having three white spots, from which the moth obtains its name of v-flava, as the spots form a minute letter v.

Now I could well understand the obscurity of the perfect insect; for who would imagine that a creature so insignificant could be the cause of so much loss and trouble to wine-owners?

It still remains a mystery to me how the moth finds its way into the cellars of our houses, or how

it can exist in utter darkness and perpetuate its
species from year to year in such a secret manner.
It is clear from the facts I have related that it
behoves all who possess valuable old wine to
examine it from time to time to see that the corks
are sound. A still safer plan would be to cut the
cork off close to the neck of the bottle and seal it
over, leaving no part of it exposed. Only in that
way, or by metal capsules, can old sweet wines be
rendered perfectly safe. I had been looking forward to the possibility of finding this minute
creature in my cellar during the spring months,
and then learning a little more about its appearance and habits, but this opportunity came sooner
than I expected. On the 20th of last December I
had occasion to go down to the wine-cellar with
a young friend who wished to search there for
various kinds of beetles, when, to my delight, I
caught sight of a minute moth upon the wall. I
could hardly believe that it was the cork moth, as
it usually hatches in April and May, but on close
inspection it proved to be the true Oinophila, and
great was the delight with which we secured the
little specimen.

The wonderful beauty of the wings could only be discerned by using a powerful magnifying glass. Seen in sunlight the little moth looked as if it were made of atoms of gold and silver, its eyes were black, its legs striped, its antennæ long, the under wings being adorned with very long silken fringes. To the naked eye the Oinophila is an inconspicuous grey object, and may well pass unobserved, especially in the semi-darkness of a cellar, and if one did remark it, the idea of destructive powers would never be suggested by anything so small and fragile.

THE CLOTHES MOTH.

"like a cloud
From closet long to quiet vowed,
With mothed and dropping arras hung."

BROWNING.

THE CLOTHES MOTH.

are all of us but too
familiar with the rav-
ages of the common
"Clothes Moth," ever busy fretting
both our garments and our tempers. We find our cherished furs
and woollens — which we fondly im-
agined we had put away so carefully
— utterly ruined by what we em-
phatically call *the moth*, as if but one species really
existed, and we refuse it our interest and our sym-

pathy. When we find some piece of material containing moth-larvæ, we are usually too intent upon destroying them to bestow much thought upon the habits of the creature; but I have discovered of late that even these moths are so curious as to be well worth a little careful study. I will relate how I came to know something about the life-history of some of the *Tineæ*, the name by which this species of insect is known.

Many years ago a friend gave me some beautiful grey feathers of birds which he had obtained during a voyage up the Nile. The majority of these feathers had been arranged in my feather-books, but a few remained in a drawer, and on examining them after a lapse of time I found they were shredded and perforated till only fragments were left. Quantities of little grey cases, or cocoons, showed that what had gained access to the feathers was moth. As I was then specially interested in the subject of domestic natural history, the living inmates of our houses, these cases were exactly what I wished to study. Accordingly I made a collection of them and covered them with a glass shade until I should find leisure

to observe them more closely. Returning from
some other occupation I found the small cases
in active motion. A brown head and part of a
white grub's body appeared at one end, and each
insect, like the Caddis Worm, was dragging its
house after it and seemed able to crawl rapidly
about. By gently pressing the tail-end of a
cocoon I made the grub come out and leave its
case behind, so that I could examine it more
particularly. The case was evidently made of
shreds of the feathers on which the grub had been
feeding, and was lined with fine white silk.

There are understood to be about thirty-one
species of Tinea in this country; of these many,
when in the larva state, inhabit fungi or rotten
wood. One beautiful species is found abundantly
in granaries, its larva lives upon corn and resides
in a case formed of wheat grains connected together by silken threads. Many of the species of
Tineina, the great group to which the genus Tineæ
belongs, are leaf-miners and form those white
streaks we may often see upon bramble, honey-
suckle, and strawberry leaves. The grubs of another kind may be found in Scotland, inhabiting

ants' nests, and even in a coal mine, near Glasgow, Tineæ have been found in abundance.

A very beautiful species of Tinea attacks the bark of the lime-tree until it becomes completely riddled by its destructive grubs. A fine avenue of about two hundred lime-trees forming one of the approaches to the town of Southampton was infested with this insect and the growth of the trees seriously injured by its ravages.

The furrier has cause to dread the ravages of *Tinea Pellionella*, which feeds on feathers and fur, and is no respecter of priceless sables and ermine. This insect makes its case with atoms of fur cut to the same length, and it works so insidiously that there is no outward sign of its evil doings until little tufts of fur begin to fall off, and then it is too late to save our valued garments. They are sure, sooner or later, to prove hopelessly destroyed.

Stuffed birds and animals can only be preserved from this annoying pest by being soaked in a strong solution of corrosive sublimate or some other poison. That this is effectual I have proved by the safe preservation of groups of stuffed birds which have hung against a wall exposed to the air without protection of any kind for the last twenty-five years; these are as fresh and bright in plumage now as when they were first obtained.

This fur-moth is perhaps the best known species in our houses; it is a small yellowish-grey insect with pale brown spots on the wings. This is, I believe, the species of which I have secured the larvæ. Fur and feathers are alike its staple diet, and it is easily distinguished from other kinds by a dark brown mark on the second segment of the grub, which mark I can discern by a magnifying glass.

The linings of chairs and sofas and the stuffing of carriage cushions, horse-hair pillows, &c., are constantly attacked by *Tinca biselliclla*, while cloth, flannel, and any woollen material, suits the taste of the almost universal *Tinea tapetzella*, against whose ravages every housekeeper has to devise a variety of protective plans. The moth is so small it can creep through minute crevices — a knot-hole at the back of the drawer or a keyhole will afford it access to the winter garments which have been put away

P

in supposed security.[1]   Tapetzella differs in appearance from the fur moth as its wings are half black and half grey, and it is also of larger size.   In laying her eggs the moth has the foresight to place them rather widely apart, so that each grub may find space enough in which to feed ; it is this habit which renders the creature specially destructive, as it attacks many parts of a garment and does not confine its ravages to one spot.   The larva of this species forms covered galleries in which it works, mining its way along the surface of the material, and eating off the pile wherever it goes and leaving threadbare tracks behind it.

Pellionella adopts a different method.   The first work of the minute grub on issuing from the egg is to form a round case in which it may live, for it does not eat unless it has a house of its own.   This curious habit may be seen in many other species amongst the Tineæ.   I have already mentioned one which forms its house of wheat grains ; another chooses particles of stone of which it constructs its

[1] It would be a wise precaution to paste a piece of paper over the keyholes of drawers in which furs are kept during the summer: the moth could not then find access to their contents if the drawers are close-fitting.

dwelling, and then feeds on the lichens which grow upon old walls. Out of the fluffy seeds of the willow one Tinea forms a sort of muff in which it lives. Other species of the group form little tents upon the leaves of the elm, oak, and many kinds of fruit-trees, these cases being so minute as to be unobserved unless the insect is moving within. One of the most remarkable of all the species is one which inhabits the leaves of the nettle. The tent looks like a tiny hedgehog, as it is formed of minute portions of the leaf glued together and studded all over with the stinging hairs of the nettle.

Mr. James Rennie in his " Insect Architecture " gives such an excellent description of the weaving operations of the Pellionella grub that I cannot do better than quote his observations upon it : " It selected a single hair for the foundation of its intended structure ; this it cut very near the skin in order, we suppose, to have as long as possible, and placed it in a line with its body. It then immediately cut another, and placing it parallel to the first, bound both together with a thread of its own silk. The same process was repeated with other

hairs till the little creature had made a fabric of
some thickness, and this it went on to extend till
it was large enough to cover its body, which (as
is usual with caterpillars) it employed as a model
and measure for regulating its operations. The
chamber was ultimately finished by a fine and
closely woven tapestry of silk. When the caterpillar increases in length it takes care to add to
the length of its house by working in fresh hairs at
either end ; and if it be shifted to furs or feathers
of different colours it may be made to construct a
parti-coloured tissue like a Scotch plaid. But the
grub increases in thickness as well as in length,
so that its first house becoming too narrow, it
must either enlarge it or build a new one. It
prefers enlarging the premises, and sets to work
precisely as we should do, slitting the case on the
two opposite sides and then adroitly inserting
between them two pieces of the requisite size.
When the structure is finished, the insect deems
itself secure to feed upon the fur within its reach,
provided it is dry and free from grease, which the
grub will not touch."

This account shows that the moth-grub can

secrete a kind of silk with which it lines its cell,
but it can use other materials out of which to weave
a house for itself. When that house becomes too
small it knows how to put in two side-pieces to
make it fit the size of its body. When full grown,
this same case forms its temporary coffin, for the
little creature simply closes up the entrance and
hangs itself up in some convenient place until in
due time it comes out a perfect moth, ready to lay
its eggs and pursue the instincts of its race. Surely
we must admit that these lives which are carried
on in our houses are very curious and worth investigation. When we think of the minute size
of these grubs (scarcely a quarter of an inch in
length) and the vigour of the instinct they display,
the secret mode in which they work in airless
drawers and boxes, the perseverance with which the
moth finds entrance into these hiding-places, we
must credit this small insect with many remarkable
qualities. Its lineage is extremely ancient, for it is
twice mentioned in the oldest book in the Bible,
and it is not a little remarkable that Job seems to
have been accurately acquainted with the habits of
the Tinea larvæ, since he says, in speaking of an

ungodly man, "*He buildeth his house as a moth,*
and as a booth that the keeper maketh " (Job
xxvii. 18).

Both of these images point to the temporary
nature of the dwelling. A booth consists of a few
branches put together at the top of a pole where a
man can sit and scare away wild animals from the
Eastern fields of fruit and grain — an erection easily
removed in a few moments; it is appropriately
likened to the moth grub's tiny case which is cast
aside after a few weeks or months, when the perfect
insect has emerged. There are seven or eight
allusions in the Scriptures to the ravages of the
moth in destroying apparel, and remembering that
Eastern people are in the habit of hoarding immense stores of richly embroidered clothing as an
evidence of great wealth, there can be no doubt
but that the many species of Tinea which are
found in Palestine were a very real danger to be
guarded against with the utmost solicitude.

THE DEATH-WATCH.

"Alas! the poor gentleman will never get from hence,"
said the Landlady to me, "for I heard the Death-Watch all
night long." — STERNE.

THE DEATH-WATCH.

CURIOUS ticking sound is frequently heard in old houses full of ancient furniture, and especially during the still hours of the night. This noise, which I often hear in my own rooms, is attributed by the superstitious to some strange omen called the Death-Watch, and even in these enlightened days there are those who imagine it to presage the approaching decease of some one in the house.

But there is nothing really mysterious about it, and it will be well for us to learn all we can about this house-dweller, so that such an absurd idea may be entirely exploded.

The sound is really caused by a small beetle of nocturnal habits, the *Anobium striatum.* This insect is of dark brown colour and rather curious form, being so constructed that it can draw its head under the thorax out of sight, retract its six legs, and thus make itself into an oval pellet. It is seldom seen by day, unless a wall may have been newly papered; to such a wall the death-watches will often flock in considerable numbers, probably to feed upon the paste. If touched, the beetles feign to be dead, and they are so brittle as to be easily injured by handling. These insects do incredible damage by boring holes in valuable old furniture, musical instruments, panels, and skirting-boards, in fact hardly anything in the way of leather and woodwork is safe from the attack of this minute pest. The female beetle seeks a crevice in old wood, and with her ovipositor places a small white egg in it and firmly glues it in a suitable position. In twenty-one days the egg is hatched, and out of it comes a white grub much resembling that which we often find in filberts. This larva begins to bore into the wood, feeding upon it, and making those small round holes we often see to our regret in some valued piece of furniture.

The grub throws out the yellow dust of the wood — often the first indication of its being what we call "worm-eaten" — and when full grown it forms a cell in the wood in which it undergoes its change into the perfect beetle.

It is difficult to convince the ignorant that the ticking sound made by this insect is nothing more formidable than the call of the beetle to its mate! It strikes its hard-shelled head against the wood, and so gives rise to the clicking sound; other *Anobiums* hear it and reply in the same way, and thus the amorous duets and trios go on, often to the great annoyance of the sleepless and suffering. Do what we will, the little torments are beyond our reach, and nothing will avail to stop the noise, though on the other hand, if we wish to set it going I believe we can do so by tapping sharply upon any wainscot where the beetles are known to exist. It is strange to read how widely the fear of this insect noise has spread in other countries besides our own. Mr. John Timbs in his interesting book, "Things not Generally Known," says:

"The superstition about the Death-Watch extends from England to Cashmere, and across India diagonally to the remotest nook of Bengal, over three thousand miles distance from the entrance of the Indian Punjaub."

The only effectual remedy for the ravages of this beetle appears to be pouring spirits of wine in which corrosive sublimate has been dissolved, into the minute holes; the spirit finds its way from one tunnel to another, and the beetles may be seen dropping out in numbers. If the piece of furniture is of large size it may require several applications to be effectual, but the process will render the wood distasteful to the insect, and probably stop its operations.

A beetle of an allied species, *Anobium tessalatum*, makes the same tapping sound in woodwork, and a minute insect, *Atropos pulsatorius*, which may frequently be found under the paper lining of picture-frames, is also credited with the power of making a clicking noise; but this can hardly be so loud as the sound of the ordinary Death-Watch beetle.

CHEESE-MITES AND FLIES.

"O would the sons of men once think their eyes
And reason given them but to study flies."

POPE'S *Dunciad.*

CHEESE–MITES AND FLIES.

T is not an altogether pleasant idea to dwell upon, that the very food we eat is sometimes tenanted by various forms of life. We can guard against meal-worms in the flour-barrel, and keep weevils from devouring our peas and beans; flies can be kept from the larder, and our dainties may be protected from the marauding cockroach; but by general consent we allow our cheese to be the home of a species of fungus, innumerable mites, and the grubs of a minute fly. Not only so, but most people prefer a Stilton or Cheddar cheese in a mitey condition, as it then possesses a heightened flavour. The first glimpse

239

through a good microscope of a mass of cheese-mites is somewhat startling. We see a confused heap of struggling insects, and the idea of eating them at our next repast is by no means agreeable. Still they are worth examination as a type of a large class of animalcules which have for their object the destruction of many substances which might taint the air and do harm if they were allowed to remain in a state of decay.

The Cheese-mite has an almost transparent oval body tapering to a snout-like head. It can move with some agility upon its eight brownish-coloured legs. In sunlight this creature's globular polished body shines as though it were made of crystal. This mite lays eggs abundantly, and also produces young alive, so this double mode of production may account for the rapid increase of the colonies in an ancient cheese.

The generic term Acarus includes a large num-ber of species. There are those which, to the dismay of the entomologist, are found destroying his finest butterflies and moths, and reducing his cherished specimens to a little heap of dust. Some special kinds of mites prey upon figs, prunes, honeycomb, sugar, and sweetmeats of various kinds. A special mite is found in the cavities of the bones of skeletons; indeed, there seems scarcely any limit to this widely-spread family of minute depredators.

Other branches of the family are represented by the Red Spider, which is one of the plagues of our greenhouses, for, although so small as to be scarcely discernible by the naked eye, it sucks the juices of plants and often effectually prevents the healthy growth of valuable specimens.

The Plum-mite may frequently be seen in clusters upon fruit-trees, puncturing the bark and doing considerable injury to the smaller twigs.

A closely allied species is known as the Harvest-bug. This almost invisible atom burrows into the human skin and there deposits its eggs, causing excessive irritation and annoyance to the workers in corn-fields.

I will now turn from the mites to another cheese-inhabitant, *Piophila casei.* Few people are likely to have noticed the perfect insect, a small black fly with whitish wings margined with

Q

black; it is very inconspicuous, and we should hardly suspect its object in visiting our cheese. When cheeses are made and placed in a room to .dry, before the outside rind has had time to harden, the Piophila will seek out some crevice in which to deposit its eggs. The creature is furnished with an ovipositor, which it can thrust out to a great length so as to penetrate to a considerable depth into the cracks of the cheese, and there it will lay as many as two hundred and fifty eggs. These hatch into white grubs without feet, but having two horny claw-shaped mandibles which enable them to bore into the cheese upon which they feed.

The breathing apparatus of the cheese-maggot is very remarkable, consisting of two tubes at the head and two at the tail, so the grub can breathe at either end of its body. Lest any particles of cheese should obstruct the front pair of tubes the little creature has the power of drawing over them a fold of the skin, and whilst they are thus closed it breathes through the air-tubes in the tail. A cheese inhabited by these grubs soon grows moist and rotten, because they have the power of emitting a liquid which softens and corrupts the cheese and renders it suitable for the food of the maggot.

The leaping power of these larvæ is truly sur- prising. Swammerdam, who seems to have care- fully studied this creature, says : " I have seen one whose length did not exceed a fourth of an inch leap out of a box six inches deep, that is twenty-four times the length of its own body." The grub can- not crawl, as it has no legs ; it must therefore progress by leaps ; this it achieves by erecting itself on its tail, which is furnished with several knobs or warts to enable it to keep its balance ; then, bend- ing itself into a ring, it lays hold of the skin of its tail, and, suddenly letting go with a jerk, it can, by a succession of springs, cover a surprising distance on a level surface. In considering the life-history of this despised creature I cannot but endorse the devout remark of the great naturalist I have just quoted. He says : " I can take upon me to affirm that the parts of this maggot are contrived with so much art and design that is impossible not to acknowledge them to be the work of infinite power and wisdom from which nothing is hid and to which nothing is impossible. It could not be the production of chance or rottenness, but the work of the same Omnipotent Hand which created the heavens and the earth."

LEPISMÆ.

LEPISMÆ.

ONG ago, I remember reading with enjoyment a little essay I met with somewhere, in which were described the various liv-ing creatures one would be likely to meet with in one's garden, if one took a stroll at night with a lantern. Beetles would be seen crossing the path, worms moving stealthily in search of food, moths hovering over the flowers; if one were quiet and still for a little time even mice and shrews might be watched foraging about bent on their own special errands.

I have indulged in such a nocturnal garden ramble occasionally, but I think it needs younger eyes than mine now are, and perhaps exceptional weather to ensure a glimpse of nature on the prowl; at any rate, I have not been very fortunate in that way. My attention during the past year has been specially directed to house-dwelling creatures, and my rambles have been carried on indoors instead of in the garden. When I think of the life-histories of the Cork Moth, of the various Cloth Moths, of the Death-Watch, of the beetles I have found at work upon the specimens in my museum, of the Solitary bees and wasps in the crevices and angles of the outer brickwork of the house, and, finally, of the creature which I am now about to describe, I think it must be admitted that there *is* a field for entomological study inside as well as outside our dwellings.

Remembering that I once caught sight of some silvery fish-like insects upon the kitchen hearth, and afterwards watched a little pair of the same kind moving below a window-ledge in a bedroom, I determined to devote a little time to their investigation. I learned that they were called *Lepisma saccherina,* and that Linnæus formed the genus, and named it from the Greek word *lepisma*, a scale. The creatures are known as "The Bristle-tails proper"; the genus belongs to the order *Thyasanura*, which contains some extremely minute but very curious insects.

Sir John Lubbock's researches have thrown much light upon the structure and habits of the *Lepismidæ*, and some of their near relations. I cannot help transcribing his description of the love-making of a couple of these atoms, known as *Smerinthus luteus*. Sir John says: "It is very amusing to see these little creatures coquetting together. The male, which is smaller than the female, runs round her, and they butt one another standing face to face, and moving backwards and forwards like two playful lambs. Then the female pretends to run away, and the male runs after her with a queer appearance of anger, gets in front and stands facing her again; then she turns coyly round, but he, quicker and more active, scuttles round too, and seems to whip her with his antennæ. Then for a bit they stand face to face, play with their antennæ, and seem to be all in all to one another."

Sir John Lubbock considers the *Lepismæ* to be

more nearly related to cockroaches than to any other form, but they do not in the least resemble those most unattractive creatures, being much smaller and of elegant shape, like slender little fishes made of silver. The body of a *Lepisma* consists of fourteen segments, the head being one, the thorax three, and the abdomen ten. The silvery scales which cover the body are so lightly attached, that a touch will bring them off. These scales have long been used as a test of power of microscopic lenses, the delicate markings on the scale being more or less visible according to the power of the glasses. The name Bristle-tail is given because of the seven caudal hairs which the *Lepisma* possesses, three of which are much longer than the rest. The Germans call these insects *Borstenschwärze* and *Silberfischen* (Bristle-tails and Silver-fishes).

Many insects seem to find wall paper an attractive diet, and the pair of *Lepismæ* I used to watch every night in the same place on the wall of my bedroom were evidently enjoying their evening meal, but as they lived in a dark corner and no very perceptible damage was done I did not

interfere ; when, however, the room was repapered
I never saw these small visitants again.

I had a great wish to keep and study these
singular creatures, and the only way to obtain
thém seemed to be by a nocturnal visit to my
kitchen hearth, where I learned they were sometimes to be seen darting about in the warmth,
seeking for such stray crumbs of sugar as they
might find.

Happily this old house is not tenanted by
cockroaches, else I should not have cared to
intrude upon their domain in the witching
hour of night ; lepismas alone were to be seen
·gliding about, but how to catch them was a
problem I found hard to solve. I tried various
methods without success, and was about to retire
quite discomfited by the exceeding swiftness of
my quarry, when a bright idea occurred to me.
With a sudden sweep of a small soft brush I
wafted the insects on to a plate, and quickly
transferred them into a glass globe. In this way
I obtained nine perfect specimens, and was able
to watch the beautiful little creatures, and admire
their glistening bodies and agile movements.

I tried to cater for their rather *bizarre* diet by giving them a little sugar and cake, some wall paper and rotten wood. After a few days they lost all fear, and would come on my hand and daintily nibble a little sugar or cake offered them; they shunned the light and kept quiet through the day, coming out for active frolics in the evening.

A German naturalist says *Lepismæ* will gnaw holes in letter paper; in fact they seem to be omnivorous, for, like the cockroach, they will eat clothing, tapestry, and the silken trimmings of furniture. This insect seems to be found abundantly in India, for a lady has told me that her garments could not be laid aside for even a few days without swarms of these "silver fishes" gathering in the folds and creases. It shares with the Death-Watch a liking for paste, and this makes it attack the bindings of books, so that it is not an infrequent tenant of the shelves of damp, unused libraries, but from its small size I should imagine it cannot do any very serious amount of damage.

Whether my specimens will develop any interesting "habits" remains to be seen; they appear to be peaceable little folk, remaining quietly in the cracks and crevices of some rotten wood during the day, and towards evening they come forth to feed, and explore the bounds of their domain. Their legs are so short they cannot climb up the sides of the glass globe in which they live; it is therefore left open at the top, so that I am able to watch all that goes on, and may learn in time something of the life-history of *Lepismæ.*

POT-POURRI.

"I plunge my hand among the leaves;
(An alien touch but dust perceives,
    Nought else supposes :)
For me those fragrant ruins raise
Clear memory of the vanished days
    When they were roses."

AUSTIN DOBSON.

POT-POURRI.

HOSE who have large gardens, and think, as I do, that the pleasure of our possessions is doubled when we can share them with others less happily endowed, may like to have ·a few suggestions as to the various ways in which our floral treasures may be passed on to the poor, to invalids, to hospital patients, and to lonely workers everywhere, who may welcome a little bit of brightness coming unexpectedly to vary the monotony of their lives. I need not touch upon the sending little bunches of flowers to the sick out of our abundant stores, since the good work done by the Bible Flower Mission is widely known, and from all parts of England the welcome hampers are sent to the various *depôts*, and find their way to nearly all our hospitals and infirmaries.

As flowers are not to be had for distribution all the year round, I should like to draw attention to other little gifts which often take their place in cheering suffering lives during the winter months. If we were obliged to live for a few weeks in a miserable garret in one of the slums of London, I suppose we might then have some idea of the pleasure that a little bag of sweetly scented pot-pourri can give to a poor sufferer who has to pass days and nights of pain in the midst of evil smells.

It is always a great delight to me to pack up a box containing eighty or a hundred of these little bags, with their pretty lace edgings and comforting texts of Scripture, and send it to some of the kind workers in London for distribution to the sick poor.

Let us follow our small gifts in imagination, and think of the gleams of brightness they will convey. There is something in their sweetness as they bring a whiff of country roses with them that must make them welcome in many a dreary room, and, more than that, they tell of other hearts caring for these sick ones, working for them, and taking thought and pains to send them little gifts.

All these things have their cheering effect, and incline the sufferer to listen to the gospel message read by the visitor from the text attached to the scent-bag, and from that will often arise an opening for helpful conversation.

The suffering one is thus led to tell of the heavy burdens that are weighing down heart and mind, and before the visit closes it may be that those burdens will have been laid on the true Burden-bearer, a humble, broken prayer telling of the link being formed between the sinner and the all-powerful Saviour.

Viewed in this light, we see of what value these gifts may be, and surely that time is not wasted which is given to preparing in the quiet of our happy country homes such things as may help the active workers in town missions who have no time to make such things themselves.

It is a very pleasant duty on a bright day in summer to go round the garden with a capacious basket and gather the harvest of rose-leaves just ready to fall and litter the ground with their pink petals. All kinds of roses will do for the purpose, and if our days were but sunny enough the leaves might be spread out in the sunshine, and would soon become dry and crisp. Unless, however, the season is exceptionally bright, I find by experience it is best to place the rose-leaves in wide, shallow pasteboard trays before the kitchen fire, and turn them frequently until perfectly dried, when they can be stored in jars ready for use.

I must give a caution against putting the leaves either in the oven or on the rack over the kitchen range, as in either case a very useless rose stew will be the result.

Where lavender bushes are available their sweet flowers may be dried and added to the rose-leaves, and dried sprays of the lemon-scented verbena will also add an agreeable perfume.

Verbena, by the way, is a plant easily grown from slips, and these, when rooted, may be planted in a southern border, or against a wall, and if matted in winter will become small, tree-like shrubs, with woody stems, and will yield a useful supply of sweetly-scented leaves for the mission pot-pourri. They are best gathered when fully matured at the end of summer. These are the chief materials required, and when the bags are to be filled I prepare the scent thus —

Taking a large hand-basin, I fill it three-parts full of rose-leaves, adding three handfuls of lavender flowers, a large cupful of coarsely-bruised cloves and allspice, half an ounce of mace (no salt of any kind), pouring over the whole about a teaspoonful of oil of lavender and another of essence of ber· gamot.

The dried gland of the musk deer, which can be had at most perfumers, imparts a delicious odour to the rest of the materials. This musk pod can be retained to scent relays of the leaves, as it will continue to give out a musky perfume for many months.

Sweet oranges entirely covered with·cloves stuck into the rind form, when dried, a pleasant addition to one's jar of pot-pourri. A stiletto is needed to make a small hole, and then the stalk of the clove is pressed in as far as it will go. If the orange is thus pretty thickly covered and then placed inside the fender where it will dry and harden slowly, it will so shrink that only the clove heads are seen ; it may then be taken for some rare tropical fruit, and when quite dried it will last for many years. The pot-pourri can be made and perfumed in a variety of ways according to taste. I have only given some general directions which I have found to answer well.

As winter comes on it is pleasant work to prepare the little bags to hold the scent. These can be quickly made by a sewing-machine, or, as in my case, enable one to keep a poor woman constantly employed to make the thousands that I need for the purpose.

Fine spotted muslin is perhaps the prettiest material to use ; any shape or size may of course be adopted, but the Bible Flower Mission requires that the bags should be about four and a half inches long by three and a half inches wide, trimmed at the open end with a narrow piece of lace about an inch wide. Special printed text cards are sold at the Bible Flower Mission Depôt, 110, Cannon Street, E.C., with a small opening in them through which the end of the bag is drawn and then tied by a little piece of bright-coloured ribbon.

I would plead with those who have the varied pleasures of gardens, woods, and fields, that they would kindly think of the utter dreariness in which thousands of our fellow-creatures live from year to year, never seeing a green leaf or bright flower, never enjoying the scent of opening buds or fragrant hayfields. Shall we not try to send some rays of sunlight into these cheerless homes, some of our bright flowers to tell of kind hearts taking thought for others less favoured than themselves? Even our dead rose-leaves will be gladly welcomed, and will last even longer than the flowers. It brings gladness to our own hearts to feel that we have been trying to cheer and uplift the weary-hearted, sorrowing, and sinful, and with our gifts let us mingle our earnest prayers that the portions chosen from God's own Word and printed on the cards may by Him be so blessed that, like seed falling into good ground, it may sink deep into human hearts and bring forth fruit an hundred-fold to His praise and glory.

A WATER BOUQUET.

Young people living in the country may welcome the following hints, which will guide them to several interesting occupations for leisure hours.

A WATER BOUQUET.

HEN flowers have been placed under water for a few hours they show a remarkable kind of beauty which can be seen in no other way. Plants, we know, are always exhaling oxygen gas from their leaves and flowers, but in our rooms and out of doors it is an invisible process. We know that this is the case from the testimony of scientists who have proved it by experiments.

We can, however, render the process visible by placing flowers under water, for we can then see the oxygen gas in the form of tiny pearls edging each leaf and petal, and streaming up in columns to the surface of the water.

I will try to describe how this effect can best be seen. Two or three well-contrasted flowers, such as a small white lily, some scarlet geranium, a few heaths, with maidenhair fern, and a little piece of arbor-vitæ, or box, to form a dark background, may be tied together, and firmly affixed by string or wire to a piece of stone.

The other articles required are a soup plate, a glass shade, and a tub full of freshly-drawn spring water. The shade should be about fourteen inches high, and wide enough to take in the bouquet we have made. The tub must be sufficiently large to allow the shade to be held upright under the water.

When all is ready, place the flowers and stone in the glass shade, held horizontally, and gradually sink it under water till the shade is quite full, place the soup plate at the open end, where the stone is, and slowly raise the

glass until it is upright, and then it can be lifted •
out and placed on a table in a window where
the sun or bright light will reach it. The bubbles
of oxygen will begin to form in a few hours,
and the jewelled effect of the bouquet will be
very curious and lovely.

It will only last two days ; after that time the
water becomes cloudy, and decay begins. The
flowers and greenery should be perfectly dry, and
the water fresh and clear, and then, with a little
dexterity, the experiment cannot fail. The remarkable beauty of a water bouquet, with its
empearled leaves and flowers, surprises all who
see it for the first time.

The fleeting flower of the night-blowing Cereus,
which opens in the evening and usually closes in
ten or twelve hours, can be preserved for double
that time by placing it in water under a glass
shade as I have described. Any flowers may be
used for the purpose, but the best effect is obtained
when only a few blossoms are grouped together,
and plenty of space is left around them.

ARTISTIC PITHWORK.

ARTISTIC PITHWORK.

HERE was an extremely artistic and beautiful model of the west front of Exeter Cathedral placed in one of the courts of the Great Exhibition of 1851 which attracted much notice and was universally admired. It had the effect of a fine ivory carving, every detail of the architecture being executed with such minute fidelity that it was difficult to believe that, instead of ivory, it had been formed entirely in pith, but of what description I could never find out.

Models of Indian temples are made by the natives from the pith of a plant called Taccada, . and our own elder-tree yields a material with which architectural details may be exactly imitated. Since, however, these two kinds of pith are not easy of attainment, I would direct attention to a source of supply which is easily accessible to those who live in the country. I refer to the common round-stemmed rush (*Juncus conglomeratus*) which grows in most places on waste lands and commons.

This plant, when the outer green skin is peeled off, furnishes a delicate white pith with which really beautiful models of Irish crosses, Gothic fonts, and other small designs may be formed. It will only peel easily when freshly gathered, so it is best to prepare a supply of the material when the rush is in perfection, about July and August, and, as the pith keeps in good condition for any length of time, it can be laid aside when quite dry, and reserved till required.

The green rind comes off most readily by beginning at the thick end of the rush and stripping it off piece by piece over the thumb-nail until all is removed. This is pleasant work to do when sitting out upon some heathy common enjoying the fresh air, and a party of young people, who generally like the occupation, will soon prepare a basketful ready for artistic work on long winter evenings.

For the help of those who would like to essay some very simple modelling I will endeavour to describe how an Irish cross, for instance, can be made which will be, when finished, a really beautiful drawing-room ornament.

The materials required are very simple and easy of attainment, viz., a quarter of a hundredweight of white modelling clay[1] and two or three wooden tools such as sculptors use.

One must have a good drawing of an Irish cross to copy from, and, if not easily attainable, a visit to the Crystal Palace will enable those within reach of London to make sketches of the crosses which are to be seen there near the entrance to the aquarium. It is well to place the lump of clay upon a dinner-plate for the convenience of moving the work when required.

The clay will shrink a good deal when dry, therefore it is well to make the model about a third larger than it is intended to be when finished.

We will suppose the cross is to be twelve inches in height. A sufficient amount of clay should

[1] To be obtained from any plaster-figure maker's for about half a crown.

be placed on the plate and gradually moulded with the fingers until it grows like the pattern drawing, the base, stem, and upper part, each to be of proportionate size.

It is best to form the whole thing somewhat roughly at first, taking pieces of clay off here and adding there, until we are satisfied that the proportion of each part is correct, and then the shaping can be more carefully done until a plain cross, smooth on all sides and perfectly upright, is the result. The model must be set aside to become quite dry, which will take a week or two, or perhaps less if it is kept in a warm room.

Some strong white flour paste or the Phastebynde paste and a small stiff brush will be needed, also a small pointed piece of wood to assist one's fingers in placing the pith upon the model will be required for the next stage of the work.

Dipping the brush in the paste, place some along the edges of the upper part of the cross, and then, selecting one of the largest pieces of pith, place it firmly on the edge of the upper part of the cross, pressing it gently to make it adhere, which it readily will if the paste is properly adhesive ; in this way a line of pith should mark out all the edges of the model. If there are panels in the pattern of the stem or arms, then the pith should be used as a moulding to keep each design distinct, and within the panels the smaller-sized pieces of pith are used to imitate arabesques or figures according to the pattern, the pointed stick being used to twist and place the material.

These are all the directions needed for a cross of simple style, like those to be found in Cornwall. The more elaborate Irish crosses with figures in relief may perhaps be rudely imitated in rush pith, but when delicate work is needed, elder pith cut with a sharp penknife would be required to make an accurate copy.

The work must be allowed to become perfectly dry, and whilst drying it should be protected from dust settling upon it.

Finally, the model should have a glass shade and will then last for years, and have the effect of carved ivory.

www.ingramcontent.com/pod-product-compliance
Lightning Source LLC
Chambersburg PA
CBHW020338030726
47496CB00007B/1931